HER SECRET WISH

By
JM Madden

Acknowledgements

As always, I have to thank my husband, because I love him more than life itself.

To Robyn and Donna, thank you for coming through in the pinch! And thank you Megedits.com for the same!

This book was a little different, in that I ran a contest to come up with the name of the hero. I had too many wonderful suggestions, but I narrowed it down to Dean Elliot West. Sharee Varilone and Elizabeth E. Neal suggested Dean Margaret Chaney Handler and Nikki Kirchenwitz suggested Elliot

And Amie Larkin Pontari suggested West

Thank you for playing lades!!!

Dedication

To all the military women out there, former or current, I commend you! Keep kicking ass!

If you would like to read about the 'combat modified' veterans of the **Lost and Found Investigative Service**, check out these books:

The Embattled Road

Embattled Hearts – Book 1

Embattled Minds – Book 2

Embattled Home – Book 3

Embattled SEAL – Book 4

Her Forever Hero – Grif

SEAL's Lost Dream – Flynn

Unbreakable SEAL – Max

Embattled Christmas

Reclaiming the SEAL

Loving Lilly

If you'd like to connect with me on social media and keep updated on my releases, try these links:

Newsletter: jmmadden.com/newsletter/

Website: www.jmmadden.com

Facebook: facebook.com/jmmaddenauthor

Twitter: @authorjmmadden

Tsū: tsu.co/JMMadden

And of course you can always email me at authorjmmadden@gmail.com

CHAPTER ONE

A S WITH MOST things in her life, Rachel could see the crash coming. It was as if time had completely stopped, but she was unable to do anything to change the events about to happen. The truck barreling in from the right hand side showed no signs of slowing for his stop sign. Even if he did manage to slam on the brakes, he would still slide through the intersection.

For a split second, she didn't know whether to hit the gas or the brakes herself. Her foot made the decision for her, slamming on the brake pedal full force. The BMW, her pride and joy, began to slow as the anti-lock brake system tried to halt four thousand pounds of forward momentum, but she knew in her heart that it wasn't going to help.

Just before the collision she clenched her body, knowing that this was going to hurt like hell, if it didn't kill her outright. As she looked up and to the right at the very last second, she caught a glimpse of the rolled iron add-on brush guard, then a flash of the man's slack face before her world exploded.

Rachel had been through several explosions in her life, both literal and figurative, and none of them had been easy. Her mother's suicide had been the first leveling blow when she was just a girl. It had taken weeks for her to come to terms that she would never see her mother's radiant face again. The second had been her father. Yes, he'd been there but he'd never been the same after the loss of his wife.

As five million things flashed through the screen in her mind before she felt the impact of the truck, she wondered if this one would be as bad as Afghanistan. At least in Afghanistan she hadn't had the killing expectation of dying she was experiencing now.

Then the expectation was gone, replaced with bone shattering force. Rachel tried to be flexible, but the rod in her spine from the last time she was destroyed didn't allow her much of that. As the truck struck the passenger side, crumpling the doorframe and blowing the airbags, she was jerked violently to the right, then snapped back to the left. As her head smashed into the window and frame, her world went spinning.

It seemed like the devastation just went on and on, her vision twirling like a top. There was a secondary crash on the driver's side, and sudden pain, then the world stilled. Rachel felt like she continued to spin, even though the world around her had stopped moving. Light splintered as it crept through the shattered windshield, sending shafts of rainbow across the jumbled interior.

Rachel was afraid to move but her protective instincts kicked in. Her eyes worked well enough when she blinked them open, although the left one had something in it. She tried to blink the obstruction away and realized it was from blood running steadily down the left side of her face. Yeah, she should have known. She'd hit that A-pillar damned hard.

She drew a breath and tried to get up the courage to move her limbs. She knew from past experience that this would hurt like hell, but she had to evaluate how badly she'd been injured. She had to know.

For a moment reality shifted and she was back in Afghanistan. Though she'd flown for most of her career, there had been times when she'd had to travel by ground convoy to one place or another. And being on the ground, watching troops get blown up, had caused her so much more anxiety than actually being in the air and looking down. It had been one of her greatest fears, being blown up like that.

Her reality re-centered to the here and now and even though it felt like she'd been blown up, she knew she hadn't.

Drawing breath was fine, but as she tried to lift her head to look around needles of pain shot down along her spine. *Oh, fuck.* She breathed deeply, trying to block it out even as fear tightened her lungs. If her back was messed up again… patiently, carefully, she lifted her head. Once her gaze was square she relaxed just a little.

With deliberate care she wiggled her toes. They were good. But her left leg was being squeezed by something and was her greatest source of pain. Lifting her arm to try to wipe away some of the blood on her face, she looked down. Her view was obstructed by the deflating airbag. She couldn't see what was squeezing her leg. Lifting her head again she surveyed the rest of her body.

There was shattered glass everywhere. It tinkled down onto her lap when she lifted her head. Scratches decorated her arms, including a nice laceration down the inner muscle of her left forearm. The blood wasn't arterial but it would definitely make her woozy if she didn't get it stopped.

Again, she tried to brush something out of her face. Ah, hell, her freakin' ponytail had come undone.

She became aware of voices outside, drawing closer. Hopefully they would look at the scene before they rushed in to help. There was a long guardrail in front of her beyond the mangled dash and she saw a couple of people climbing out of their vehicles to gawk.

Glancing around she tried to find something she could wrap around her arm. Her gym bag had been on the back seat but she doubted there was any way she could reach it. The distinctive pinging sound of a message being received on her phone registered, but she couldn't see the unit itself.

Taking another breath she knew she had to straighten herself up in the seat and try to do an assessment. That way, when first responders arrived, they'd all be that much ahead of the game.

Swallowing her fear, she gripped the steering wheel in front of her and used it to help her lift her chest. She'd expected searing pain but she actually only felt bruised discomfort. Nothing clicked or ground together like a broken bone. As soon as she was vertical, her breath began to come easier.

Oh so carefully she swiveled her head to the left and the right. Everything *seemed* to be working okay.

The BMW had come to rest against a guardrail on the east-bound side of the road. She'd been heading westbound. It was amazing that she hadn't struck someone head on. There were a few cars directly in front of her, the drivers staring at her open mouthed. If she could have laughed and waved, she would have.

Her left leg throbbed with excruciating pain. Pushing the deflated airbag out of the way she tried to see again what was restraining her but couldn't.

In the distance she could hear sirens, several of them, and she wondered what had happened to the guy in the truck. Her car had surely taken the brunt of the damage. With that huge brush guard on she doubted he'd even felt hitting her expensive little car.

There was a scrabbling outside and a few voices lifted in alarm.

"Are you okay in there?"

The deep voice came from the back of the car but Rachel didn't swivel her head to look; she was still being cautious. "Y...yeah." She cleared her throat. "I'm fairly okay."

"Good. I'm trying to get to you. Just hang tight, okay?"

Rachel choked out a laugh. "Sure. I'm not going anywhere," she promised.

There was a scrabbling in the back of the car again, then a pounding. The car shook around her as if someone were trying to break into the vehicle.

"What's your name, ma'am?"

That deep voice was incredibly calm. It stood out from the concerned yammering of the onlookers.

Then his words registered. Rachel would have laughed if she'd been a little more with it. *Ma'am? Really?*

"Rachel. Searles."

"I wish we could have met under better circumstances, Rachel." His voice strained as if he were lifting something. "My name is Dean. Dean West. I'm on Denver PD. First responders have been called and they'll be here any minute. We'll get you out, okay?"

"Okay," she whispered. "My left leg is trapped. Otherwise, I seem to be intact."

"Well, that's good to know."

Rachel rested her head against the seat, adrenaline making her muscles quake. She wanted to bolt. *Think about something else, damn it.* "Is the other driver hurt? I saw the crash coming but couldn't do anything about it."

Dean's voice was muffled. "Nah, I think he'll be fine. His vehicle is a lot beefier than yours."

"Mm," she murmured. She blinked, wondering why it was so hard to keep her eyes open. The blood loss? "Hey, Dean?"

The car rocked again, as if he were trying to rip the passenger side door open. "Yeah, Rachel?"

"I think I'm going to pass out, honey."

There was a pause in the jostling of the car and then it started up again in earnest.

Rachel let her eyes fall shut and hoped Dean managed to get it open.

DEAN CURSED AS her voice went quiet, her head lolling forward at an awkward angle. Blood-stained honey blond hair hung forward over her face. Sweat began to bead his forehead as he tried to wedge one of the doors open but it wasn't working. The woman had been struck in the passenger side but the driver's side was wedged against the crumpled guardrail. The expensive black BMW had been totally crunched. There was no way to get into it. Wait. The most intact part of the vehicle was the hood. Careful of the buckled edges, he climbed up onto the hood, lying on his stomach. The windshield had been shattered and glass glittered all over the inside of the car.

The woman didn't move when he said her name. Daring to reach through the obliterated windshield he searched for her carotid artery in the side of her neck. The beat was there, though a little fluttery and faint. "Rachel? Rachel."

She didn't move. Dean looked down her shoulders and body. There was a slice down her left arm but he couldn't see anything more than that. Scrambling for something to stop the bleeding he looked through the car, but didn't see anything. "Shit," he muttered.

Sitting up on the hood of the car he stripped off his orange Columbia t-shirt, folding it in half. Leaning back down he wrapped the fabric around her arm, trying to put pressure on it without hurting her.

Long dark eyelashes fluttered and her eyes opened, then winced in pain.

"I'm sorry, ma'am. We need to put pressure on this to stop the bleeding."

Golden eyes the color of warm caramel lifted to his as if it were the hardest thing in the world to do. Dean grinned at the woman, trying to be reassuring.

"Oh, damn. You're too cute for your own good," she mumbled. "And look at those muscles. Hmmm."

Dean laughed but didn't let up the pressure on her arm. "Thank you. Try to keep your head still, okay?"

An ambulance pulled to a stop right beside him, silencing the siren. "Rachel, your ride is here." Reaching up he ran his thumb over the arch of her left brow, wiping away the blood. Though his training screamed for gloves before he made the action, some visceral urge overwhelmed his common sense.

Her eyes flickered but she didn't turn her head. "I'll take your word for it. You're going to have to pull the car away from the guardrail before I can get out, though."

Dean felt a trickle of fear roll down his spine. "Why Rachel?"

Blinking, trying to brush at the blood on her temple, she moved her chin toward the floorboards. "My left leg is trapped. Gonna need something to wedge it out."

A paramedic caught his attention and Dean repeated what she'd just said.

"Fire department's on the way. They'll get her out. Can you squeeze over a little?"

Dean did as he was asked but didn't let release the pressure on her arm. Rachel's eyes flicked to the paramedic, then back to his own as if she didn't want to lose the connection. Dean didn't want to either. Even as the medic asked her questions, she continued to look at Dean.

"Your eyes are amazing," she sighed.

Dean gave her a brilliant smile. "Thank you. I have to say, yours are too. Like caramel that's been left in the sun to melt."

A cell phone chimed from inside the jumbled car and she choked out a laugh. "I can't come to the phone right now…"

Dean laughed with her, trying to encourage the lightheartedness, in spite of the situation. "If it's important they'll call back."

"Yeah," she sighed, her eyes closing. "Maybe you can find it for me if I get out of here."

"*When* you get out of here, not if," he corrected.

But she didn't respond. "Rachel?"

Things began to move fast then. After he checked her vitals the paramedic working on her managed to fit a cervical collar around her neck and began bandaging her arm. The firemen arrived and it was quickly decided to use hydraulic extraction tools to get her out of the car. Dean told one of the guys what she'd said about her leg and he nodded, stepping up on top of the hood with the huge Jaws of Life machine.

Dean relinquished his hold on her arm to the paramedic and stepped away from the car to give the firemen room to work. But he watched Rachel through the mangled passenger door.

Nathan Killian, another DPD patrol cop and his best buddy, stopped beside him. "Did you see this happen, West?"

Dean nodded and quickly scanned the area. "Unfortunately. Where's the truck?"

Killian shook his head, shrugging his shoulders. "It totally disappeared. We've got several units canvassing the area. If it was decked out like you said, he may not have even sustained any damage."

Dean nodded, fuming. It was bad enough the woman got hit but the second vehicle leaving the scene of the crime was criminal, literally. "Let me know if you find him, would you? I'm going to stick with her for a while. I'll tape a statement for you tomorrow morning when I'm back on duty."

Killian nodded and returned to diagramming the scene.

Dean made sure to stay out of the way of the first-responders. He knew from experience that there was nothing more aggravating than trying to do your job around rubber-necking civilians. But when they finally pulled her from the car a half hour later, he waded over to the gurney heading to the ambulance. She had regained consciousness, her eyes fluttering in the sunlight. Leaning over her he blocked out the sun so that she could focus on him. "See, you made it out."

"Yeah," she sighed, eyes drooping closed.

Dean let them load her up, watching closely as they locked the gurney into the back of the vehicle, closed the rear doors and took off.

CHAPTER TWO

✦

S TUNNING AQUAMARINE EYES with mile-long lashes plagued her dreams and as soon as she woke, she wished she could go right back to sleep. Doctors and nurses were poking and prodding her. Somebody walked into the room holding blue x-ray films and the group paused to huddle around it.

"What did I break?" she asked.

One of the young men in the circle turned to look at her. He grinned, looking a little clownish with big glasses perched on his skinny-ass nose.

"Ms. Searles, glad to see you awake. We're just looking at your scans. Looks like you've been through some trauma before."

She sighed, wishing she could turn the overhead lights off. She couldn't even turn her head away from the light because of the cervical collar. "Yes. A bit," she told him, totally tongue-in-cheek.

He turned back to the scan and even she could see the long metal rods in her spine, as well as the half a dozen fixators and twelve screws, showing white on the dark blue background. "Mid-back fracture, T4, 5 and 6 several years ago. Helicopter crash in Afghanistan," She explained.

Her Doogie Howser doctor turned to look at her, eyes bugging behind his glasses. "Well, luckily for you there doesn't seem to be any damage to the prior repairs, although I'll forward these to an orthopedic surgeon to make sure."

The ball of tension in her stomach eased but she wondered if she should even listen to the kid. He looked like he'd just graduated high school.

A second, more mature man stepped to the side of her bed, reaching to remove the collar. "I don't think you need this anymore. I'm Dr. Carter. Can you tell us what happened?"

Fighting impatience, Rachel went through the series of events as she remembered them.

"Excellent. And what day is it?"

"Saturday."

"That is correct." He pulled a penlight from his pocket to shine into her eyes, then away. "You have a concussion from your head striking the doorframe of the car. While it's not too bad, I don't think I want to release you just yet. Head trauma can be unpredictable. You've got severe contusions on your left calf but again, no breaks. We had to put a dozen stitches in your arm, but those can come out in a week to ten days. I think you were very lucky this time, Ms. Searles. The airbags protected you from the worst of it."

Rachel wasn't ever going to bitch about spending so much money on that car, then. The airbags alone had probably saved her from extensive injuries to her already compromised body. She could spend the night in the hospital. It was so much less than she'd expected.

Several hours later she was ready to bitch. Though they were only doing their job, the damned nurses would not leave her alone. As soon as she drifted off to sleep, which she needed desperately, they slipped in to check her pupil response and other neurological markers. After she'd been woken up four times in the course of the evening, she snapped at the pretty brunette twig with the perma-smile. "If you people don't leave me alone for the next six hours to get some real sleep, I will walk out of here AMA. Do you get me?"

Her shiny perma-smile wilted. "I don't know if I can do that."

"Then you better check with whoever is in charge because even though this bed is one of the softest hospital beds I've ever felt, I will walk out of here without hesitation."

They gave her four hours. Barely.

As Rachel cracked her lids open to look at the woman pushing a wheeled cart into the room, her eyes flicked to the clock on the wall. Four hours would be all she would get today. Although, if she went home she could sleep all she wanted.

With that thought in mind, she demanded to be released as soon as the doctor came for rounds. And though he hemmed and hawed, he eventually gave in in the face of her implacable stubbornness. The doctor gave her a handful of prescriptions and demanded that she follow up with her general practitioner. Rachel promised she would because it was only sensible. She didn't want to have any more medical issues than she had already.

As they wheeled her down the long hallway to the front of the hospital, she wondered who she could call to come get her. Maybe if there was a valet they could call her a cab. Shit, she didn't have any money. She was just wondering if it was still possible to make collect calls when the orderly wheeled her outside the doors.

There was a white Denver PD cruiser waiting at the curb, with an aquamarine-eyed savior in uniform leaning against the fender. For a moment, Rachel just had to stare. She'd known the man had to have been real, but she'd never expected to see him again. And she certainly didn't remember him being so gorgeous. Or so *built*. Those muscles had taken many long, long hours in a gym to achieve, but he wasn't muscle-bound. Those incredible biceps strained the sleeves of his shirt but weren't *too* much.

As the orderly pushed her wheelchair to the turn-around, the hunk in the black uniform pushed away from the car, lips spread in a blinding smile.

"Were you in uniform before?" she asked, confused.

The officer shook his head. "No, ma'am. Yesterday was my day off."

"Yet you still ended up working."

He shrugged his incredibly broad shoulders, giving her a sheepish look. "It was worth it to help rescue a beautiful woman."

Rachel barked out a laugh, truly amused. "If you think a blood-covered face is beautiful, you may need to seek help."

Dean laughed with her, head tipped back and strong column of his neck moving. Though he wore a bullet-proof vest beneath his uniform, Rachel could tell he moved like a trained warrior. She was stunned to find herself so drawn to him. Though she worked with gorgeous, confident men every day, it was work. The fact that Dean had shown up here, appearing to want to give her a ride and check up on her, made her think this was more personal. Maybe she should clarify. "Do I have a statement I need to fill out or something?"

Dean blinked those glorious eyes. "Well, that's up to your investigating officer. I signed out to give you a quick ride home. A buddy's wife works here so she called me when it looked like you were getting out. She said you were a bit of a pain last night."

His gaze did a quick head to toe, taking her measure, then his smile broadened.

Rachel was a little stunned. Men weren't generally drawn to her. It had been pounded into her head that she was too strong, a little too butch, to appeal to men. After being in the military for so many years, and especially in the exclusive group she'd been in, it had not benefitted her to be feminine, so she'd tried to block that part of herself away.

"I...thank you for the offer of a ride, but I can call a cab."

Dean shook his head and moved forward, holding a broad hand out to help her from the chair. Rachel took the offered hand without thinking, letting him lift her up. At any other time she'd have brushed his offer of aid away and just shoved up out of the chair herself.

Something about Dean West had knocked her world a little off kilter.

His strong hand gripped her own and tugged but she swayed. She took a step to steady herself and ended up chest to chest with her rescuer.

Rachel stepped back, flustered, and angry with herself that she felt that way. What the hell was going on with her? Maybe she could blame being so out of balance on the pain meds they'd given her.

Dean still had that ornery grin on his face, but it seemed to be tinged with awareness now. Surely that couldn't be right... no man in their right mind would go for her, not looking the way she was right now. The nurse had apologized when she'd handed over Rachel's bag of dingy, blood-streaked clothes. There was a monster bandage on her temple, where she'd had to get a few stitches in one of the lacerations. Her hair hadn't even been brushed in a solid day, let alone clean.

Rachel didn't have family in the area so there was no way she could have fresh clothes dropped off. She could call one of the guys from LNF, but she didn't want anybody to know what had happened if she could avoid it. Although in the interest of full disclosure, she should probably let Duncan know what had happened.

"Let me drop you off somewhere. As long as you don't mind riding in the cruiser, I can save you some cab fare."

Rachel gave him a narrow-eyed look. "Do I have to ride in the back?"

Dean chuckled deep in his chest. "Not today. I'll let you ride in front like a big girl."

His humor was pretty contagious. And she didn't live far from the hospital. She wouldn't put him too far out of his way. "Fine. Lead the way, Officer West."

Without another word he took her elbow in his hand and walked her carefully to the car. He jumped forward enough to swing the door open for her, then grabbed a couple of things off the seat and threw them through the hole in the glass partition to the back seat. It was incredibly sweet but a little off-putting too. That back seat had probably seen a lot of fucked up things.

Rachel settled into the car seat and reached for the seatbelt, but he'd already stretched it out and was leaning in to reach around her hips to snap it shut. Blood suffused her face—she could feel it. Even as tan as she was, he had to see her embarrassment. "Thank you," she choked out.

Rachel didn't know if it was because she was so embarrassed or what, but it seemed like he withdrew *very* slowly, giving her an incredible amount of time to look at the dark blond stubble growing in on his square jaw. When he finally pulled out of the car and carefully shut her door, she heaved a breath. *Holy hell, what the fuck had that been?*

Officer West circled the front of the car, giving her a chance to catch her breath and give herself a stern talking to. Yet as he settled behind the wheel, his broad shoulders reaching beyond the width of his seat, she had to wonder why he was taking the time to be with her.

"You didn't have to do this," she murmured.

That broad smile turned her way. "I know. But I wanted to. I wanted to check and make sure you really were recovering."

Okay, that time she didn't imagine it. Dean West had held eye contact with her way too long. Blinking out of her own daze, she watched his strong, broad hand twist the key in the ignition and shift the car into drive. Rachel took a moment to look at the interior of the car. Dash mounted pc, cursor blinking. Miscellaneous papers stuffed into the sun visor above his head. A spare set of cuffs hanging from the spotlight at the left of the dash. Typical patrol car; although spotlessly clean.

"How long have you been a cop, Mr. West?"

His blond head turned, one brow raised. "About seven years. I graduated police academy a year after I graduated college. Been on the job ever since. I moved out here from California about six months ago to be closer to family."

He was still unbearably enthusiastic about his job. Rachel sighed, feeling older than her actual years. It had been a long time since she'd been that eager about anything.

"So, how do you feel? Nothing broken obviously, but you've got to have been beaten up."

Rachel sighed. "Yes. My left calf is hugely swollen and tender, but no major damage. I was injured in the service but even those prior injuries were fine. I was lucky, I guess."

West looked at her, interest in his eyes. "Which service were you in?"

"Marines," she told him with a small smile. "I was a helicopter pilot."

Yep, there it was. That slack jawed look people always got when she told them where she'd been for the past several years.

"Wow, that is very cool."

Rachel gave him a nod and turned to look out the window. It had been cool. It had been the coolest thing she'd ever done. Well, besides fly.

That familiar need to be soaring through the blue surged through her. It had been a couple years now since she'd been behind the stick and she missed it like hell. She looked up at the puffy clouds in the sky today. Optimal flying weather.

"You have a faraway look in your eyes. I can tell you miss it," he murmured.

Rachel blinked and sighed. "Yes, I do. More than anything."

"Can you not still fly?"

She shrugged and turned to look out the window without answering him.

Luckily, he didn't pursue that line of questioning.

"Do you know how the other guy was in the crash? Was he injured?"

Dean gave her a look out of the corner of his eyes. "Actually, we haven't found the guy who hit you. He left the scene."

Rachel felt her mouth drop open. "Are you serious? He hit me and took off?"

Dean gave her a sympathetic look. "Yes, he did, but we have people looking for him. We're checking the surveillance footage of the convenience store a mile down the road to see if anything's there. I got a vague description but I was too far back to get details. There was a lady ahead of you that stopped and had more info, so we're trying to piece everything together. We'll find him."

Rachel sank back in the seat, her aches and pains bone deep and with no closure on the accident to help her put it into perspective. Damn it.

Dean pulled into her neighborhood and drove to her duplex

without direction. It was nice to have a cop drive you home. No directions needed. As they pulled up in front of her garage door, Mrs. Lightner, the widow next door, flicked her living room curtains and Rachel knew she'd be having company soon, whether she wanted it or not.

Dean parked the cruiser, hopped out of the car, and circled the hood to open her door. Rachel waited, though it chafed her independence a little. But honestly, she didn't think she'd be able to push up out of the seat without serious assistance.

Or…was she just yearning to touch Officer West again?

Dean opened the door and held a hand out to her. Rachel took it and swung her legs out, then braced herself on his hand to stand. That solid anchor never budged as she gained her feet and she appreciated that more than she could have expressed. "Thank you," she sighed, waiting for her bones to settle before heading for her door.

"Oh, wait," he told her, ducking back into the car. The trunk popped and he went around to retrieve a white plastic bag. "Here are your keys from the car and your wallet and cell-phone."

Well, duh… how the hell had she planned to get into the house without her keys?

"Thank you so much, Dean. My head's been so foggy with the concussion and stuff I didn't even think about my things." She flipped open her handy, dandy cell phone case slash wallet. All of her cards were inside, as well as the cash she'd had. She hit the power button on her phone.

"I turned it off to save what battery you had left. It was beeping a lot."

Rachel cringed when she saw all the messages and missed calls. "Yeah, I work with a pretty protective group of guys. I was supposed to go work out with a couple of them yesterday. I'll call them back."

Even as she finished speaking the phone vibrated in her hand with another incoming message. Maybe she shouldn't have turned it on just yet.

Dean walked beside her as she limped her way up the sidewalk to her door then waited while she unlocked it. Rachel turned a little uncomfortably, wondering how to gracefully say goodbye. "Thank you, Dean. I appreciate everything you've done for me. Really. You've gone above and beyond."

He shrugged away her thanks with a smile. "You don't have to thank me. But if you'd like to do something for me, maybe you'll agree to go out to dinner with me?"

Speechless, Rachel blinked, shock coursing over her. With her unclean everything—clothes, hair, face, mind—her heart raced with embarrassment. The man was sex incarnate and she was in the nastiest state she'd been in a long time. Was he hoping she would give in because she was feeling vulnerable?

When she didn't say anything immediately, he waved a broad hand. "You don't have to answer now. Take your time. I know I should have waited until you were a little more recovered, but I couldn't help myself. Just think about it."

Giving her a look that seemed a little embarrassed, he headed back down the driveway.

Rachel's heart raced. And just the fact that she had such a physical reaction to his request made her open her mouth and call out a 'Yes'.

Dean looked back at her and grinned. "I can call you?"

Giving a single tight nod, Rachel tucked her hair behind her ear before backing into her condo.

Gasping, she dropped back against her door and covered her mouth with her hand. What the hell had she just done? There was no sense pursuing this…flirtation.

CHAPTER THREE

D EAN VIBRATED WITH excitement all day, wondering how
long he needed to wait before he called Rachel Searles. If
he called too soon, she'd know what a geek he was, but he didn't
want to put it off too long because he wanted her to know how
interested in her he was.

As he backed into the driveway of a derelict building, one of
his favorite spots to catch speeders, he glanced at the empty seat
beside him. Though she'd been embarrassed and in pain, he'd
loved having Rachel beside him. When he'd touched her, his
skin had prickled with awareness.

Rachel had an allure for him that he couldn't figure out. She
wasn't the prettiest woman he'd ever seen, but she was definitely
the strongest. It wasn't very often that he met a woman who
impressed him that way, but she definitely did.

Her face was lean-boned and her golden eyes direct, full of
knowledge about a life lived on her terms. She was tall enough
that he didn't feel like he was going to break her if he hugged
her, and strong enough that she looked like she could take him
down if she felt she needed to. The thought of grappling with
her sent a bolt of longing through his cock.

Dean's shift dragged on. He'd sworn to himself that he
would give her a day to recover but as the hours crawled by his

determination flagged and he got a little out of sorts. The speeders he pulled over probably wished he was having a more relaxed day because he listened to every convoluted excuse then wrote them out the ticket.

He drove back to the substation, gathered his crap and locked the car. Then he strode into the building. There was only one report to write but several tickets to forward to the courthouse. Killian slapped him on the back as he walked into the building.

"You working out tonight, West?"

Dean nodded. "Yup. I'll be there."

He seriously needed to work off some of this anxiety.

RACHEL CALLED DUNCAN. After she spoke with Shannon for a minute to give her the scoop on what had happened, her friend connected her to the boss of LNF.

"Wilde," he answered.

For some crazy reason, emotion suddenly attacked her. It took several heavy breaths to calm her unease. "Sir. I'm just returning your call. I'm sorry it took so long. I was in a car crash."

"Are you okay, Searles? Do we need to come get you?"

Rachel swallowed hard in reaction to his words. The solidarity that every Marine had was so irreplaceable. "No, sir. It happened yesterday. I spent the night under observation for a concussion, but they released me this morning. I'll be into work tomorrow."

"Damn, Searles. Are you sure you're okay to return? You can have some time off if you need it."

"Thank you but no, sir. I'm pretty sure I can be in tomorrow."

Come hell or high water, she murmured to herself.

"Well," Duncan told her firmly, "if you change your mind, stay home. Sometimes the effects are the crash are felt more later on."

Rachel choked out a laugh. "Oh, I doubt I can feel much worse than right now. In the spirit of full disclosure I should probably tell you they had to cut me out of the car."

There was a long pause on the other end of the line.

"Shit, Searles! Was this a single vehicle or did somebody hit you?"

"Somebody hit me. Then drove off. DPD is investigating but I doubt they'll find him. Totaled my car."

"Damn," he breathed. "That sucks. That was a nice car."

She laughed, a little wistfully. "Yeah, it was."

The car would have to be replaced, too, and as soon as possible. She could ride her bike in the meantime. Assuming she wasn't too sore to move tomorrow.

"Take tomorrow off. That's an order. And I'll leave it open in case you need more time."

Rachel sighed, knowing it was probably best. She wouldn't do anyone any good if she had trouble moving in the morning. "Okay, I'll stay home. Thank you, sir."

"Quit feeling guilty, Searles. Stay home and get better. I'll work your ass harder when you come back."

"Agreed."

She hung up, exceedingly thankful she had settled in Denver, Colorado. The Lost and Found Investigative Service was incredible. Duncan Wilde had created an environment open to any and every type of former military, as well as any and every type of disability.

When people cycled out of the military, either retired or medically discharged, the servicemen and women were usually left at a loss as to what to do with themselves. The skills taught and encouraged in the service were not necessarily applicable to civilian life. And if they were wounded, or *"combat modified"*, it made it that much harder to find a slot to fit in.

Wilde had created a company that didn't necessarily *cater* to their wounded employees, but did definitely make allowances for, and adapted to, their new lifestyles. He still required that they all attain their private investigator's licenses and conduct themselves in a business-like manner, as well as perform physically to the best of their abilities. No matter what their disability, every man and woman at LNF played on level ground.

It was exhilarating. And not something she ever wanted to jeopardize for any reason. She had enough sense to know, though, that she could be more of a liability and distraction at work tomorrow than a help.

DEAN WAITED TWO endless days to call Rachel, though it almost killed him. Six o'clock. He could call her after six. After his shift had ended and he'd gotten home. But the benchmark had been distracting as hell. Even the guys at work remarked on his being distracted, but he couldn't help it. Thoughts of Rachel plagued him, until he wondered if there was actually something wrong with him.

The little piece of paper with her number on it sat on the coffee table in front of him, but he didn't need it. He'd long ago memorized what was on it. The note was just comforting to have.

As he punched the numbers in to his cell phone, he had to pause to clench his quaking hand. Forcing his fingers to move, he finished the sequence then waited, breath held, for her to answer.

But she didn't answer.

Disappointment swamped him and he had to shake it off. Even as he debated calling her again, the cell phone rang in his hand. Heaving a breath, he swiped a finger across the screen. "Hello?"

"Hello. Is this Dean?" The voice was tentative.

"Yes! Rachel?"

"Yes," she chuckled. "Sorry I missed you the first time. I couldn't move as fast as I needed to grab the phone."

"No big deal. Really. I didn't wake you, did I?"

"No, I'm up. Achy. Trying not to take the pain pills they gave me."

Dean could totally sympathize. "I was in a motorcycle wreck a few years ago. Destroyed my right ankle and messed up my knee. I can understand not wanting to take the pills. They knocked my butt out and made me dizzy. And nauseous."

"Yes, that's exactly what they do. And I'm bored out of my mind. When I get like this I usually go work out but the doctor said I have to lay off that for a week."

That sounded like an opening if he'd ever heard one. "Can I bring over some takeout? We can play cards or I can stop and rent a couple movies."

"Oh," she sighed, and he could tell she was thinking. "Yeah, that might be okay."

Though it wasn't the rousing 'hell, yeah' he'd hoped for he'd take it. "Okay, I'll be over in about an hour."

"Sounds perfect. Later!"

CHAPTER FOUR

A N HOUR. OKAY. What did she need to do in an hour?
Settle her nerves, first off.

With that thought in mind, Rachel went to the kitchen to make herself a cup of tea. Grunt, her feline roommate, looked at her with mild reproach as she moved around. Though his food bowl was mostly full, enough had been eaten that he feared starvation, apparently. Crossing to the cupboard with his dry cat food, Rachel very carefully leaned over, back straight, and drew it out of the depths. Pain shafted through her spine as she raised herself up. She decided then to leave the canister on the counter.

Rachel looked around the house. Though she wasn't a messy person there were a few things she needed to pick up. She went to the bedroom closet and reached up to the top shelf, searching. There it was. She pulled down the long aluminum stick of the gripper tool. It was only about three feet long, but it kept her from having to bend over.

Moving slowly through the house she picked up the items she needed to and lit a candle. Though she couldn't decorate worth a damn she loved to have candles around. Maybe the yummy smell would make up for sitting on the plain brown furniture.

Glancing at the clock, she winced. Dean would be here within forty minutes. The thought of having a man she didn't work with in her space was very strange, but a tingle of feminine excitement ran through her. It had been months since she'd been out on a date, and she certainly hadn't been excited before, during, or after that disaster.

Rachel showered and cleaned up, then took the time to add just a bit of makeup to her eyes. She'd never been one to use a lot. As she looked at the bruising and small line of black stitches at her temple, she wished she'd have listened to one of her girlfriends when they'd tried to teach her. There was a bottle of foundation in the basket beneath the counter, but when she opened the lid she realized it had dried out. Grrr…

Moving to the bedroom, she stood in front of her closet doors. If he was just bringing over some pizza or something, she didn't need to go all out but maybe more than jeans and a T-shirt. Dragging the hangers along the rod, she debated what to wear. Her hand hovered over a nice apricot colored button down shirt, a little more feminine than what she normally wore. Mentally shrugging, she slipped it on. It would have to do.

Running some pink gloss over her lips and scraping her hair back into a ponytail she moved back out to the living room to stare at the clock. Anxiety hit her then. Was this a date? Kind of?

Dean arrived right on the dot of seven, knocking firmly on the door. Rachel's heartbeat took off and she blinked at the sudden tension in her body. Deliberately taking a deep breath she moved to pull open the door.

Dean grinned as soon as he saw her, his vivid aquamarine eyes crinkling with emotion. "Hello, Rachel."

"Hello, Dean."

Lifting his pale brows, he ran his gaze over her face. The man got brownie points for not looking at her chest. But then she kind of wished he would because his direct, drawn-out examination was making her a little uncomfortable.

"You look amazing. I hope this didn't stress you out too soon after the accident."

Rachel made a face and gave a slow shake of her head. "No, I'm fine. Believe me, I've dealt with more stress than this. Come on in."

She stepped back to let him cross the doorjamb and into the room. There was a brown paper take-out bag in his huge right hand. "I hope you like Mexican. I've got this great place down the block from my apartment that I go to way too often."

Rachel was surprised. "No, Mexican sounds delicious, actually. Not what I expected."

He shrugged his broad shoulders. "I didn't want to take the easy route, you know, like a pizza."

Grinning, he crossed to her dining room table and started unpacking Styrofoam containers. He set a second brown paper bag aside then set a foam clamshell at one place setting, and a second at the other.

Rachel watched the heavy muscles of his shoulders flex and extend as he unpacked the food. She was around men every day, had been her entire life. She had always been a better guy friend than girl friend because she didn't get into all the girl stuff. If asked whether she'd like to shoot or shop, shooting would get her vote, hands down, every time.

But as she looked at the way Dean moved, lean back elongating as he reached across the table, she decided she didn't want to be his buddy. At least, not *just* his buddy. *God, he had a great ass.* She jerked her attention back to what he was doing, barely escaping notice as he turned to her.

"What can I get you to drink? Beer, pop, water?" she asked, hoping it covered the blush on her face.

"I'll take a water, please."

Rachel drew two tall glasses of ice water from the filtered jug she kept in the fridge and walked them to the table. Dean looked up at her as she entered the room and she almost stumbled. The look in his eyes… it took true strength of will to set the glasses down without spilling the water.

He actually moved to hold the chair for her. Face burning, Rachel let him scoot the chair under her butt. "Thank you," she murmured.

Dean sat across from her and the chair actually creaked. His eyes flicked to hers and he widened his eyes theatrically. "I've only destroyed one chair in my life, I swear!"

Rachel laughed and looked away, entirely too charmed by him. "It's stronger than it looks. Though you are a big dude." She took the excuse to look him up and down.

He wore a soft blue button-down shirt, short sleeves revealing his muscular biceps and forearms. Dark blond hair covered his tan skin and her gaze could trace the length of his veins down his arms. She wanted to trace those same veins with her fingertips.

Dean leaned his head down to catch her gaze and Rachel felt her skin heat again. Shit, he'd caught her gawking at him. "Yes?"

He tipped his chin toward the white Styrofoam container in front of her. "I ordered chicken fajitas and enchiladas. Which would you prefer?"

They both sounded good. Hunger was suddenly overriding the nausea. "Can we split them?"

Dean's perfect smile spread and he nodded, putting her request into action.

"Where are you from, Rachel?"

"I'm from a little bit of everywhere. My dad's in the Marines, so we bounced around a lot. I'd been to more countries by the age of twelve than most people see in their lives. My dad is getting ready to retire in a couple years. He'll probably stay in Pensacola, where he's stationed now."

"With your mom?"

Rachel stared at him for a moment before shaking her head. "No, my mom committed suicide when I was about ten."

Dean cringed and reached forward to rest his hand on hers. "I'm so sorry. I shouldn't have asked."

The touch of his cool fingers on hers made her appreciate him all the more. "She got tired of the life, I think, though she never told Dad that. We were getting ready for another move out of the country when she swallowed a bunch of sleeping pills."

Though she didn't say it out loud, she had been the one to find her mother, of course; lying on her bed as if nothing were wrong. It was not unusual for mother to take a lot of naps, which when she got older Rachel realized was a symptom of her ongoing depression. But Mom had always been good about getting up to make dinner for her daughter and husband. That night she did not.

"Did you have brothers or sisters?"

"No, just Dad. But after Mom…left, he was a very different man. She had been the central support of our family and when she left things fell apart. My dad used to be a steady fixture in my life, but he couldn't stand to be at the house without Mom in it. He got the acceptance he needed from the Marines, and I mean that literally. He was on base as much as possible."

"I'm surprised you weren't a little resentful of them, then."

Rachel nodded. What an interesting insight. "No, not resentful. I graduated high school and joined the Marines myself as soon as I could. For a while I found that acceptance, too. Dad was proud of me for a while. There's nothing like knowing the guy next to you will take a bullet for you."

Dean lifted his brows at her as he shoved a forkful of food into his mouth.

"Oh," she laughed. "I guess you do know. How about you? Do you come from a long line of cops?"

Dean tilted his head. "You know, I didn't used to think so. My dad is a carpenter and all of my uncles did construction work, but a few years ago I learned from my mom that her family had been heavy into law enforcement. That must be where I got the urge."

"And does your family live around here?"

He nodded. "My dad's been having health issues so I moved back here to be close to them."

"Where were you before?"

"California. I had gone to college out there, loved it, and never left. One of my workout buddies was an Anaheim cop and everything he did sounded fascinating. So, though I have a degree in computer programming, I went to the police academy and worked there for years. I loved it. I just moved here to Denver about six months ago."

Rachel quirked an eyebrow. "Sounds like you had fun out there."

"I did," he told her with a grin. "But Dad's getting older and I needed to be close for Mom."

The food was probably as good as he'd promised, but she didn't taste any of it. She was too busy watching him. Light brown stubble darkened his jaw but his skin was nicely tanned, obviously from being in California. It was also obvious he worked outside a lot. He had the typical cop sunglass tan, paler around his stunning eyes.

Dean moved seamlessly from one topic to the next and managed to keep her entertained throughout the meal. He had an unending supply of 'crazy-ass suspect' stories and she giggled more than she had in a long time. It was nice not dwelling on losing her parents. She hadn't talked to her dad in a long time because he felt she'd taken the easy way out with the medical release. Whatever.

Dean told her a lot about himself—likes and hobbies—but she sensed there was so much more to him. Rachel wanted to ask him a million questions but didn't feel it was exactly appropriate at that time.

She sat back in her chair, surprised at all they had in common. They each had a love of speed and riding the edge of danger. As one of the few women to fly the heavy Super Stallion helicopter in combat she wouldn't have given that experience up for anything. It had been the most trying but rewarding thing she had ever done. Dean talked about law enforcement the same way.

The two of them also had a love of physical fitness and an eagerness to experience all life had to offer. When he mentioned the motorcycle he'd crashed she took him out to the garage to show him her bike. The black Honda 250R was a few years old but definitely suited her need for speed...occasionally.

"I had a Ninja 650R. That thing was a beast," he sighed, face going soft with remembered enjoyment. "But it got away from me on a rainy night. I've been thinking about getting something new to replace it."

There had to be several years' difference between them, but everything he talked about she enjoyed. "How old are you, Dean?"

Again, that ornery grin. "I'm twenty-nine."

A few years younger than her, not much, but miles apart in experiences.

Rachel wanted to act more reserved, but there was no way. She was enjoying talking with him too much.

"Tell me about the military."

She lifted her brows in surprise. "Well, I was in there for ten years, all told, before I was shot down. I flew the Super Stallion, a heavy equipment and personnel helicopter. I could haul 55 troops or thirty thousand pounds of cargo. Or if it was a slung load, up to thirty-six thousand pounds. I hauled Humvees and armored vehicles all over Afghanistan."

He blinked in amazement. "That's incredible. Truly. I've been near those things and they are impressive. Massive machines."

"Yes, they are. It was a great time in my life," she admitted. "I still miss it."

He nodded, eyes going thoughtful. "I would miss running hot if I couldn't do it again. And just helping people."

Rachel nodded. "I know what you mean. That's one thing I love about LNF. We do that there."

"If you have a job that you can feel fulfilled and like you're helping the community; that really makes a difference in your well-being."

It did, truly.

Rachel took a more comprehensive look at Dean. Yes, he was handsome and virile but he had a depth to him that she didn't always see in men. Coming from the military environment she'd been in, she'd seen more than her share of egotistical jocks. Dean had the build and character to dominate any situation if he wanted to, but he didn't. Everything she'd seen him do had been compassionate and gentle. And he didn't seem to feel the need to *act* like he knew everything.

"I agree, whole-heartedly," she smiled.

That direct gaze dropped to her mouth and it was all she could do to keep her lips curved.

"You're a beautiful woman, Rachel."

The smile completely fell away as arousal swirled through her. Damn, it had been a long time since anyone had stirred her that way. She'd heard the words before, many times, but when they were thrown at her as an attack, questioning her ability to do her job or how she'd gotten there, the effect had been very different.

Dean wasn't belittling her or trying to get sexual favors from her in the middle of the desert.

Taking a heavy breath, she tipped her head. "Thank you, Dean. I appreciate that."

He glanced at the clock on the wall and started gathering up trash. "As much as I've enjoyed this I should probably get going. You're still recovering."

Rachel also glanced up, amazed to see that it was after ten o'clock. She didn't want him to leave. She was enjoying herself and had totally forgotten about her pain and boredom.

Piling everything in the paper bag he started to put it in her trashcan, but it was too full. Setting the paper bag aside he pulled the plastic bag full of trash out of the can, settled it against the floor a couple times and put the paper bag inside. "Where's your trash can?"

She motioned out the back door to the wheeled Waste Management container, a little humiliated that Dean was hauling out her trash, but also fascinated. Damn. A good looking guy with conversation skills, unending sexiness and an openness to clean. What the hell?

Dean laughed when he caught her looking at him and moved close enough to look down at her. "I took the trash out but you can put the bag back in." Then he seemed to reconsider his words. "Wait, where are your trash bags?"

"Left hand cupboard under the sink."

Sighing, he moved to pull a folded bag from the roll, snapping it open before he settled it into the trash can. Then, moving back to her he leaned down to drop a kiss to the top of her head. "I only did it this time because you're injured and I didn't want you to bend over. I can tell how stiff you are. Next time it's your turn."

He pointed a meaty finger at her, then gathered up his phone and turned to leave.

Rachel followed him to the door, her bones creaking. The huge man took up a lot of room in her home but she hated to see him leave. "Dean, thank you so much for the dinner and everything. I really do appreciate it."

"Thank you for seeing me. I hope it doesn't seem too strange." He cast her a squinty look in question.

She shook her head, what she could. "Not at all."

"Think we can do it again, but maybe go out next time?"

Rachel blinked, a little caught off guard. "Yes, I guess we can. Call me."

That broad grin stretched his mouth again and she had to catch her breath. Before she could move away he leaned in and brushed his lips over hers. Rachel gasped but he'd already pulled away and was slipping out the door.

As she watched his broad back heading to the black truck in the driveway, she had one of those premonitions. There was another crash coming. This time straight to her heart.

Being a woman in the Marines had made her leery of men. There were too many incidents of sexual abuse, both reported and not. It had been common practice to go everywhere with a buddy—shower, latrine, chow hall. Rachel had never allowed herself to be in a compromised position. Every relationship she'd taken part in had been deliberate and on her terms.

The emotions Dean stirred in her were definitely *not* on her terms.

CHAPTER FIVE

D EAN HATED TO leave. When she'd opened the door and
he'd seen her standing there, his tongue had glued itself to
the roof of his mouth. When he'd picked her up at the hospital,
she'd cleaned up a little, but damn. Now that she'd removed the
big bandage and gotten some sleep, she looked flippin' gorgeous.
He'd had no idea.

But her expressive eyes had still carried a lot of pain.

Everybody had issues to deal with in life. Rachel seemed like
she'd had to deal with more than normal, especially after her
service in the Marines. Dean wanted to wrap her in his arms and
hold her on his lap, curled under his chin as he blocked out the
world and gave her a chance to recover.

As he slid into the cab of his truck, he looked back at the
house. She stood backlit by the living room lamp, a thoughtful
smile on her face.

Though she hadn't said it outright, he knew she wasn't wild
about the few years' age difference between them. It didn't mean
anything to him, really. The woman was incredible. She hadn't
gushed about herself like a lot of women he'd met out here. And
she certainly didn't make herself out to be more than she was.
There were a few pictures throughout her condo, one of which
was of her in her flightsuit standing next to a small group of

other women in flightsuits. Her hair had been a lot shorter then, but she'd still been stunning.

Dean felt a pull to Rachel that he'd never experienced with any other woman. From the slightly dazed look in her eyes when he'd kissed her he hoped she felt the same.

Killian teased him unmercifully the next day as Dean agonized over whether or not to send her flowers. "I don't think she's into flowers." He frowned, looking at the pages of options on the computer in front of him.

"All women are into flowers," his partner told him.

Killian didn't even look up from filling out his paperwork, so he missed the skeptical look Dean sent him. Then he did jerk his head up. "Hey, there's a place in Arvada that sends those edible arrangements. I bet she likes cookies or fruit."

Dean thought about it for a minute. "That may not be so bad."

He found the place online and placed an order for a mixed arrangement of brownies and cookies.

Killian grinned at him as he pushed away from the desk, paperwork in hand. He smacked Dean on the shoulder. "Hopefully she won't think you're criticizing her weight."

Dean looked up at him sharply. "No way. She wouldn't, would she?"

Killian shrugged his heavy shoulders. "You never know with women. They're strange creatures. I've been married eighteen years and I still haven't figured my wife out. When she starts yelling, I just apologize. Then I get her flowers."

Dean gave his buddy a look. His wife Joyce was one of the most pleasant people he'd ever met. He doubted she'd ever lifted her voice to her husband at all.

Killian must have seen the look on his face because he grinned, his blue eyes shining. "Okay, I may be messin' with you.

I love her to pieces and we get along better than we ever have. Now that the yahoos are getting older and more self-sufficient, we have more time for each other. She's really sweet right now because she wants to do another cruise this year. I'm going to soak up the lovin' then give in, but not just yet."

Dean laughed at the wicked light in his buddy's eyes. Killian had been his training officer when he'd first moved out here last year, and they'd been the best of friends since. They traded insults and jokes almost constantly, but Dean knew if he ever needed anything Killian would be right there.

Dean gave him a serious look. "Rachel appeals to me more than any other woman I've ever met. It's a little scary how similar we are."

Killian grinned at him crookedly. "That's excellent! Good thing you weren't working that day, huh?"

"I know."

If there were an active case it was kind of an understood rule that there could be no fraternization between the officer in charge and the subject. Too much chance to lose objectivity. But Dean wasn't worried about that.

Even if he had been the officer doing the report he doubted he would have been able to resist asking her out.

RACHEL WENT BACK to work on Wednesday. Wilde had talked her into staying home an extra day, probably because he'd heard the pain in her voice. She was too stubborn to take the pain pills they had given her, but she would take the time off, then make up her workload later.

When she walked into the gleaming office building that morning, Shannon was waiting for her. The smaller woman dared to reach out and wrap Rachel in a careful hug. "I was so worried about you. Are you okay?"

For a moment, Rachel was a little choked up. She wasn't aware she'd meant that much to Shannon. Yeah, she'd been incredibly welcoming, but hadn't she done that for all the new hires? Maybe it was just because she was pregnant now and everything seemed to make her emotional.

"I'm fine. Just bruised and sore."

Shannon turned her left arm over and gasped at the line of stitches. "Oh, fuck!"

She slapped a hand over her mouth and looked down the hallway guiltily, scanning for Palmer. "I told John he had to start laying off the word fuck because the baby is coming, and now I've said it."

Shaking her head, wincing, she released Rachel's hand. "When did this happen?"

"Saturday."

"And they had to cut you out with the Jaws of Life? Is that what I heard?"

Rachel nodded and pulled out her cell phone to show Shannon the picture of the mangled car. Dean had taken it for her. The smaller woman's eyes filled with tears. "I'm sorry, I don't mean to cry." She reached out and gave Rachel another hug. "If I had known, I would have been there for you. I know your family isn't nearby."

Incredibly, Rachel's throat began to tighten. Shannon was so sweet to have said that. "Thank you, Shannon. Honestly, I was kind of out of it for a while, then I slept the rest of the night. When they released me, I kind of had a buddy waiting. There was a guy that stopped, an off-duty cop named Dean West. He got there right after I crashed and helped me out, then he picked me up when they released me from the hospital."

Shannon's sharp hazel eyes turned considering and Rachel

felt her cheeks flush. She was a decorated Marine, had flown in several deployments, but the look Shannon was giving her made her feel like a junior high school girl talking about her first crush.

A slow smile spread Shannon's lips and she reached out to squeeze Rachel's upper arm. "If you ever need to talk, I would love to have lunch sometime."

Rachel blinked and looked at Shannon in fresh consideration, thinking about the dried up make-up under her counter. Some girly interaction might be nice. "Thank you. I may take you up on that."

Grinning, Shannon nodded and returned to her desk.

Wilde rocked back in his chair and crossed his arms when she walked into his office. She tried not to limp too badly, but she could tell by his contemplative look that she hadn't fooled him. "You're moving under your own power at least."

Rachel nodded. "Yeah, hurts like hell but I'm up."

"Well, if you think you need to go home early let me or one of the other partners know. We're slow enough right now that your absence won't cause too much inconvenience."

"Thanks, Duncan. I appreciate that."

Wilde gave her an assignment investigating a series of strange bank deposits in a client's account. It was necessary work but not physical.

When she left and went into the break room a few minutes later she had to show the guys the long line of stitches on her arm and the bruising that enveloped her calf. The ribbing that she got for her 'boo-boos' started up and she loved it.

DEAN CALLED HER two nights later as she was settling into her recliner.

"I was wondering if you'd like to go out with me tomorrow."

Though he wasn't here, she grinned like an idiot. "I would love to. Thank you for asking me."

"Do you have any preferences about where to go?"

She thought for a moment. "You know, I actually don't. I'm up for anything."

"Okay, well, I'll pick you up tomorrow at six."

"Sounds perfect."

Rachel stared at the phone in her hand long after he'd hung up.

IT HAD BEEN a long week but Saturday had finally arrived. Thoughts of Dean had plagued her in everything she did. Though their contact had been minimal, she was absorbed with wondering what he was doing. She knew cop work, but what did he do when he wasn't on duty?

Unable to help herself she walked to the bedroom. The swelling had gone down on her temple and she'd already tugged out the stitches, which her doctor would probably yell at her about. The bruise on her leg had changed ten different colors, but it was slowly starting to fade. Another week and it would probably be gone completely.

The stitches in her arm, on the other hand, bugged the shit out of her. The skin beneath them was healing, creating an itch. She left them open to the air when she was home, but covered them with a bandage when she went out. She was on the verge of cutting them out as well but the laceration there had been deeper.

As she looked through her closet now, wondering what the hell to wear, she debated just pulling on one of her workout tank tops. They were super comfortable and practical. Definitely not date material though.

Rachel settled on a little frillier blouse in shades of blue. It had been a spur of the moment purchase a couple years ago, still had the tags on it, but it seemed okay for tonight. Maybe she'd talk to Shannon and see if they could go shopping sometime. Her wardrobe needed a serious overhaul.

The shirt chafed when she put it on and she remembered why she'd never worn it. Just for tonight she could put up with a little aggravation to look a little prettier for Dean.

But the longer she wore it the more determined she became to go shopping with Shannon.

CHAPTER SIX

D EAN DIALED KILLIAN as he drove toward Rachel's house. "Hey, I'm heading over to take Rachel out. Any suggestions on where to take her? I don't want to go to the Mexican place down the block from my apartment. She needs something nicer. A date place. I had planned to take her to a movie, but that's so lame."

Killian was quiet for several long seconds. "I've got the perfect place for you to take her. It's not very big but it's a classy joint. It's called the Pink Cactus."

Frowning, Dean jotted down the address Killian gave him. "Okay, sounds interesting."

"Great little Tex Mex place, but a little higher end. You'll love it!"

"Okay, thanks buddy. We'll try it."

Dean glanced at himself in the rearview mirror as he parked the truck. Damn, he'd missed a spot shaving. He ran his thumb over the patch of bristles under his chin. Hopefully she would be too enthralled with his good looks to notice the little spot. Yeah, right...

Rachel opened the door almost immediately, as if she'd been waiting for him to knock. Dean tried to control his surprise, but every time he saw her she was more gorgeous. The bruising on her head had faded and she'd done something to her hair to make it curl around her face. Wow, no ponytail. She was wearing the prettiest shirt he'd ever seen her in and he wondered if she'd gone shopping for tonight. Rachel seemed most comfortable in BDUs and a T-shirt top.

But her expression was the most interesting. There was trepidation there but also true excitement. Unable to help himself he grinned at her and leaned in for a kiss.

Dean would have settled for just a peck right now, but she surprised him by leaning into his touch, just a bit. Damn, she felt good.

One of his hands drifted up to cup her cheek and she let him brush his thumb over her skin. "You taste better than my dreams," he admitted.

Rachel leaned back enough to give him a sharp look, but her eyes drifted back down to his lips as if she couldn't help herself. There was no way he could say no to that invitation, so he pressed his mouth to hers again. Sharp arousal slid down through his gut and into his groin, shocking him.

Dean had kissed a few girls, but probably not as many as people thought. Yeah, he knew he was a decent looking guy, but dating had never come easy to him. There had never been that one person that just did it for him.

Rachel was making him wonder, though.

When he pulled away she blinked up at him a little hazily, and he was gratified to know that he wasn't the only one affected. "Are you okay?"

She nodded, tucking her hair behind her ear. "Yes." She paused to clear her throat. "Just surprised me, is all. Guys don't usually...well, that was nice."

What had she been about to say? Guys didn't usually kiss her? Like her? Accept her? As he looked at her tentative gaze, he

J.M. MADDEN

wondered what it had been like in the Marines for her; stories floated around, good and bad. He would ask her about it in a bit, if it felt appropriate.

"Are you ready? My buddy told me about this great place on the south side of the city."

She nodded and grabbed a light jacket from beside the door. She grabbed her keys and cell phone wallet then pulled the door shut behind her. "I am."

Dean walked her to the truck, very aware of the heat of her body beside him. He opened the truck door for her then waited till she slid inside. She reached up to grab the overhead handle and he caught himself staring at her lean, rounded bicep, revealed by the frilly sleeve of the shirt. Damn! The woman had some guns on her!

He circled the hood of his truck and slid behind the wheel. Dean started the engine and pulled out of her driveway. "So, you've got a great build. Where do you work out?"

"At work, actually, Lost and Found. All of the guys there are former military and very into physical fitness. We're not real big, but we have a gym in the office."

Dean was impressed. "I can tell you use it."

Incredibly, her cheeks flushed with color. "Yeah, I do. I was very active but after the helicopter crash I had to immerse myself in rehab. I don't have the range of motion I used to, so I can't fly any more. I tried to rehab myself back into my job, but it didn't work. I had to take a medical discharge."

Glancing at her, he tried to read her flat expression. He had a feeling it hurt a hell of a lot to go through that, and not just physically. To have the military turn you out because you couldn't do the job anymore, even though you were trying, had to hurt. "Being an investigator is cool, though, too. Maybe not as exciting as flying huge helicopters but it has to be interesting."

44

A smile spread her mouth. "Oh, it's definitely more interesting than I expected. I've only been here a few months and I've already been shot once and helped foil a kidnapping and attempted murder."

Dean turned to her, trying to tell if she were telling the truth or not. "Are you serious?"

She nodded and tugged up the bottom of her shirt. Dean thought she was showing him the lean planes of her tan stomach but she pointed out a long white scar on her left side. He glanced up to the road, then back down to the scar. "Damn! That sucker is huge!"

Rachel grinned. "Yeah. Fucking burned like fire too. I was fighting a guy and he got off a shot. I didn't even realize he'd hit me until I took him down and managed to catch my breath."

Dean looked at her with fresh eyes, totally impressed. "I know I keep saying it, but *damn!*"

She shrugged and motioned ahead of them.

The car in front of him had slowed dramatically and he had to hit the brakes rather sharply. "Sorry," he muttered. "You are a total badass. I already thought you were but the more I get to know you the more impressed I am."

Rachel winced and shook her head. "Don't be impressed. I'm just doing my job."

As much as she protested, he knew Rachel Searles was an incredible woman, and he couldn't wait to learn more about her.

The GPS voice gave them directions to the Pink Cactus. It was only about ten miles away but far enough outside his district that he was fairly unfamiliar with the businesses.

As they neared their destination and he prepared to for the final turn, he glanced over at Rachel. For some reason she had her hand over her mouth. Her eyes glittered with laughter. "What?"

She pointed a long finger up through the windshield.

Dean looked up at the sign and could have choked. "What the hell is that?"

The sign said Pink Cactus, but it was the picture next to it that made him shake his head. He assumed it was a pink cactus, but it had two spikey cactus paddles and one large…paddle, in the middle. From a distance the sign had a very hairy, very phallic look to it.

Rachel was doubled over in her seat, tears streaking down her cheeks as she laughed. "I'm sorry," she gasped, chuckling. "I just didn't expect it to look so…male."

Choking, Dean pulled into the lot and parked in front of the business, but something wasn't right. "I don't think this is even a restaurant."

They climbed out of the truck and walked to the front, then along the sidewalk to the plate glass window decorated with the phallic cactus. Rachel leaned forward and cupped a hand over her eyes to peer into the depths of the store. "It's women's clothes," she gasped, disintegrating into giggles again.

"What?"

Dean leaned in and looked for himself. Yes, indeed, it was a women's clothing store. They definitely had a western flair, hence the cactus. He grimaced as he caught sight of one of the price tags on the rack of clothes inside the door. Even those were decorated with the phallic cactus.

It hit him suddenly. "Killian did this. He knew what it was. He just wanted to embarrass me."

Dean pulled his cell from his pocket and hit the dial button when Killian's name popped up. His partner answered with just a couple of rings, and he was already laughing.

"Dude, what the hell?"

Killian cracked up on the other end of the line, laughing

uncontrollably. It got a little quieter as if he'd moved the phone away, but after a few seconds he came back. "Hey, buddy, what's up?"

Dean knew it had been meant in fun, but it still grated on his pride. He was here trying to impress a woman, maybe *the* woman. "The Pink Cactus, really?"

Cackling on the other end of the line, Killian lost his shit again. Dean looked at his phone, frustrated. "Really?"

Then the acoustics of the phone call changed. Two Denver PD cruisers pulled into the lot and their drivers stepped out. Killian was one of them. He circled the hood of his car, hands held out placatingly. "It was just a joke, buddy."

The other officer, Noah Burns, circled his car to pound Dean on the back. "We knew you hadn't worked much in this district. Don't be too mad at him, West. All the newbies get sent here eventually."

Shaking his head, Dean turned to look at Rachel. Her skin was flushed with delight and her golden caramel eyes sparkled with fun. She seemed totally okay with the situation.

All of the aggravation he'd felt at having the joke played on him washed away. If it made her smile, it was totally worth it.

Then she reached out, resting a cool palm on his forearm. It sent a shock across his skin and drew his focus straight to her. "They're just playing. I'm not offended at all. Actually, I think we need a picture."

That was how he found himself in the middle of the parking lot with a giant, prickly, pink dick the backdrop to a selfie of the four of them.

He couldn't resist dragging Killian into a headlock, though, and wrestling a little. "Just you wait, *Buddy*. You are so fried. I don't know when or where, but you have retribution coming."

Killian wiped tears from his eyes and pounded Dean on the

back when he let him go. "I know, West. I can't wait." He turned to Rachel and held out a hand. She took it immediately. "I hope you know we were just yakkin' it up with our boy. He's a good man, putting up with all the ribbing we've given him since he hired on."

Rachel grinned and shook his hand before releasing it. "No, you're totally fine. I get it."

Dean leaned in to catch his buddy's eye. "She's a former Marine and works at that detective agency on the East side, Lost and Found."

Killian's eyes widened. "Oh, hell. Well, you know all about the ribbing that goes on with the newbies then."

Rachel nodded, her eyes shining.

"I've been a cop for years," Dean groused.

"Not here, you haven't," Killian corrected. "Hey, one of the detectives were able to decipher the plate from the surveillance cam at the quickie mart. They picked up the guy today and impounded the truck. Thought you'd like to know that."

Rachel appreciated that he'd remembered to tell them. The truck had been a loose end niggling at her mind. "Thanks, Killian. You just made my night that much better."

He grinned, enjoying her praise.

Their radios came to life and both of the uniformed officers' concentration sharpened, then they turned for their cars. Burns keyed his mic as he climbed behind the wheel and took off, siren screaming. Killian was right behind him.

"That was abrupt," she commented.

"Domestic case, they had to go."

Dean watched them disappear down the street, his own heart pounding with shared exhilaration. He loved his job.

CHAPTER SEVEN

✦

R ACHEL LOOKED UP at the rapt expression on Dean's handsome face. There was an excitement radiating from him that she recognized in herself from years ago. She'd had the same expression every time she'd looked at the Super Stallion, twenty-four million dollars' worth of ferocious machinery ready to carry her troops into combat.

And though she'd only just started with the investigative work she could see herself loving it just as well, in a completely different way. Would she ever fly helicopters again? Probably not. But she could modify her life to make it as thrilling and fulfilling as possible.

Dean had that look in his eyes. That look that said he could do his job happily for twenty-five years and retire extremely satisfied with his career. That confidence in what he was doing was so appealing. "Have you wanted to be a cop all your life?" she asked him.

His grin turned rueful. "How could you tell?"

"It's that little boy look on your face."

Shrugging those wonderfully broad shoulders he gave her a single nod. "Ever since I was a kid. I have pictures of me in a uniform when I was just little."

"That's very cool," Rachel murmured. "My grandfather was

in the Marines, too and I grew up listening to his battle stories."

Nodding again, they moved toward the truck. "I don't know about you but I'm still hungry. I do know of a restaurant a little north of here called Dazzle. Are you up for it?"

"Absolutely!"

They settled into the cab of the truck and belted themselves in. Dean started the truck and moved into traffic. Rachel watched his hands move on the steering wheel, a little entranced. He drove confidently, aware of everything around him. She wondered if he would make love the same way.

Definitely.

As he turned right, the muscles in his arm bunched and released, teasing her. Rachel wanted to reach over and explore, but it was too early for that. Right?

Her body urged her otherwise. Time to focus on something else.

"You know Killian was just ribbing you, right?"

He glanced at her out of the corner of his brilliant eyes. "Oh, I know. He was totally looking for my reaction. But I was a little disappointed too, because I thought it would be a nice place to take you."

She waved a hand. "I'm sure where ever we go will be fine. I'm not picky."

A few minutes later they pulled into a parking spot near the eatery. There were already customers heading in the door. "They don't open till four on weekdays but they have phenomenal jazz. Hope you don't mind."

Rachel smiled. "I'm open for anything."

Dean looked at her with narrow-eyed consideration then took her hand in his. Rachel knew it had to be a test so she kept her hand there, enjoying the closeness that was beginning to build between them. Dean was everything that she always imagined she would like in a man; tall, well built, and exceptionally kind. As they walked into the bustling restaurant, he held the door open for an older couple, then felt he needed to hold it for the party of eight that came next. If it wasn't for a gentleman a shade more polite than Dean who ordered him inside, Dean would still be standing out there. But as she looked at his happy expression she could tell he would have been fine holding the door all night if he felt he was the man to do the job.

As he walked toward her where she waited just beside the hostess stand, his expression changed, became more watchful, more aware. Then his gaze drifted oh, so slowly down her body. Rachel had been waiting for him to do the completely male action the entire time she'd known him. It was as if he had waited until he knew she would catch him then she could see the carefully banked desire he'd been hiding. As she looked at the appreciation in his eyes, she vowed to go shopping for clothes that would actually flatter her.

Rachel's heart began to race. She'd never had a man look at her like that before and it was a little shocking how her body reacted. Beneath the shirt and bra her nipples drew into hard peaks and a seductive warmth curled through her belly, then drifted lower. Moisture slicked her palms with nervous, anticipatory energy. She wanted to get up close and personal with Dean West but worried that he would find her naïve and inexperienced.

Yes, she'd slept with men before, but more to get her virginity out of the way than anything. She'd heard about some of the sexual abuse cases in the military and knew there was no way she was going in a virgin. As crazy as it sounded, she wanted to make the choice of who she gave her virginity to; Grant had been a nice guy but definitely no long-term prospect, perfect for what she'd wanted.

The second guy she'd slept with had been more because she'd wanted him. They'd crossed paths on base a couple of times and when they'd come together it had been more fun than she'd expected. They'd continued their affair for a couple of months until he'd been shipped home. She'd been sad but certainly not heartbroken. They hadn't had that kind of attraction.

Dean, on the other hand, thrilled her on many different levels. They hadn't gotten close to getting naked, but she had a feeling that when they connected, it would be making love rather than just having sex. The man was impossibly delicious.

When he stopped in front of her, in spite of the people swirling around them, he cupped her face in his palms. "For that look alone, you could ask the world of me right now, Rachel Searles and I would do my best to give it to you. What is your secret wish?"

The breath caught in her lungs and emotion suddenly tightened her throat. Yes, she was a strong woman, used to taking care of herself and doing what needed to be done but sometimes she would just like to give up control to someone else. Someone who would keep her best interests at heart and protect her through everything life threw at her. Was that too much to ask for?

He was waiting on an answer and she didn't know if she dared tell him what she wanted. What if he laughed in her face at the crazy request or sidestepped her answer? He was such an exceptional guy she didn't understand why he hadn't been snatched up already by some other needy woman. Cops ran across women in distress all the time. What made her special? Why had he made it a point to take an interest in her life?

Maybe she *should* tell him exactly what she wanted. That way, if he bolted now he wouldn't shatter her heart. She was into him but not so much that she would try to hold onto him if he wanted to walk away. At least, she didn't think so.

Straightening her spine, she took a deep breath and cupped her hands over his. "I want a man who will respect me no matter what. I want a safe haven where I can relax my guard and not be expected to carry the weight of the world on my shoulders alone. I want someone who will hold me in the night when the nightmares of crashing, over and over again, wake me."

There was a confident smile on his lips, as if she hadn't said anything he wasn't willing to give her. "I want a man that will take care of my heart as if it were his own."

Dean smiled and leaned closer. "Done," he whispered, before moving in for a kiss that made her gasp. Rachel knew there were still people moving around them. She was a little embarrassed at the display they were putting on, but she couldn't pull away from him.

Dean's mouth opened over her own and his tongue slipped out to taste her lips. Rachel groaned, opening for him. French kissing a man was not her favorite thing to do, but Dean did it *wonderfully*. As his slick heat invaded her mouth and Rachel leaned into the exploration. Reaching up and around his shoulders, she angled her mouth to fit more solidly against his. One of his hands settled on her hip, tugging her tight against him.

"Ahem, you're kind of blocking the aisle way. Excuse me!"

Rachel would have ignored the irritating, voice but Dean pulled away, reluctantly it seemed. The black pupils of his glorious aquamarine eyes had expanded, telling her that he was seriously aroused. She would have known that without seeing his eyes though. With a final, gentle nudge against the erection she could feel against her hips, she stepped away, tugging her shirt into place.

The hostess stared at them tapping her toes in aggravation. "Your table is ready."

She led them to a tiny table against the far wall, barely big enough for them both to fit.

"I think this is revenge for blocking her traffic flow," Dean muttered.

Rachel grinned, agreeing, and opened the menu. Then, with her face hidden, she tasted her lips. God, she tasted like him now, spicy and minty.

When the harried waitress came around she ordered ice water and a grilled Alfredo pizza. It made her mouth water just reading the ingredients. Dean ordered a California burger.

"I love avocado," she murmured. "That was my second choice."

"Well, when she brings it I'll let you have a bite."

"And I'll share my pizza, of course."

Rachel sat back in her chair, a little amazed at the conversation. They sounded like a married couple, together for years and used to sharing food from each other's plates.

"You are very comfortable for me to be around, Dean," she told him honestly.

He winced a little. "Comfortable? Not exhilarating? Or stimulating? How about arousing?"

Rachel grinned. "You're all of those, actually. And more, but comfortable is the most important, because it leads to the others."

He gave her a narrow-eyed look. "You're very comfortable for me to be around as well, Rachel."

The waitress brought the food more quickly than Rachel would have expected considering how crowded the restaurant was. And Dean did exactly as he had said. As soon as the waitress left he gathered up the monster burger and offered her a bite. Rachel almost told him no but he seemed to be testing how comfortable she was with him. Leaning forward she took a healthy bite. Then had to sigh in pleasure. "Oh, wow, that's really something."

Using the spatula to scoop a piece of pizza, she made a motion for him to move his hands. She set the slice of pizza on the edge of his plate and he grinned. Then she put one on her own plate and dug in.

The restaurant was as incredible as Dean had promised, but Rachel barely noticed. She was more interested in watching Dean—the way his bright white teeth cut through the meat of the burger, the strong way he chewed. It was ridiculous the things she was noticing, like the tiny little mole on the edge of his right jaw bone.

The good news was he watched her as much as she watched him.

They made it through dinner chatting about inconsequential things. It was pretty amazing to realize how similar their lives were. They'd both moved to Denver within the past year. Both loved to work out with friends and play around, but they both had rock-solid work ethics.

And they were incredibly drawn to each other. Anticipation hummed in her blood and she wondered where the night would end up. She never imagined she would be a woman to go home with a man the night of their first date, but she was beginning to rethink those personal boundaries.

After paying the bill, they wandered through the trendy area around the restaurant, going from shop to shop and talking about the things they observed. Dean would hold her hand as they crossed intersections, then he wouldn't let go unless she made a move to pull away. He made it a point to be affectionate without being clingy.

Rachel found she was the one wanting to be clingy. As they wandered through a tiny little artisan shop, she had to force herself to give him space as they shuffled through the narrow aisles. When they stepped back out into the cool night, Dean tugged her to the edge of the walk and kissed her. Rachel let her hands settle on his hips, her heart racing. Dean was the only man in a long time who didn't make her feel awkward as hell. At five ten, she stood as tall as, or taller than, many men she knew. She'd been taller than most of her flight crew, which had been a point in her favor, actually. Height coupled with strong personality very often correlated to being the person in charge, which completely worked for her.

Dean, on the other hand, she did not need to manage, and she thoroughly enjoyed the fact that he was several inches taller than her. As they walked along the street now, he rested his left arm along her shoulders, then seemed to think better of the movement and pulled away. "Sorry, did that hurt?"

Rachel shook her head. "No, not at all. I just feel a little strain down through there right now."

"What happened? Do you mind me asking?"

"I took heavy fire over Afghanistan and it was all I could do to get back to the forward operating base in Jalalabad. We landed hard enough that we wrecked our landing gear and hit dirt. Thirty-three thousand pounds in the sand. It could have been worse, but several of us were injured pretty seriously. I broke several vertebrae from the force of the hit. We had lots of broken bones and strains. Funny thing was they had to fly us out on a helicopter because of our injuries. Talk about getting right back on the horse that bucked you off!"

Dean winced and shook his hand. "Damn. You've survived a lot. Do you miss it?"

Rachel grinned softly. "I do, in spite of all of the hardships we had over there. In spite of being swiss-cheesed, I got all my guys home safe and mostly in one piece. I'm held together by plates and screws but it could have been so much worse."

She leaned into his strong shoulder. "Yes, I miss it all the time, but not enough to go back to it."

Dean pulled her close, pressing a kiss to her unbruised temple.

They walked in silence for a good while, just enjoying the night and being together. Dean fit to her side like they'd been made for each other.

Eventually they circled back to his truck. He unlocked it and held the door for her while she slid inside. But he didn't pull away. Instead he leaned in close, his eyes parallel to her own. "I want you to know what an incredible night I've had, better than any other date I've ever had."

As she looked at the sincerity in his face, she knew he meant every word. "I did too, Dean. Thank you for a lovely evening. I haven't..." She looked away for a minute to order her words. "I am not a typical woman. I'm too strong, too independent, not what most guys go for."

Dean lifted his brows and leaned in to drop a kiss on her nose. "It's a good thing I'm not like most guys, then, huh?"

A soft smile lifted her lips and her eyes actually moistened. "Yes, it is," she agreed. "Take me home, Dean."

With a final lingering kiss, he pulled away and carefully shut the door, but his eyes stayed locked on hers. Rachel felt exposed but somehow liberated as well. Was this what it was like to be in love? Having all your secrets exposed, yet accepted?

When he climbed into the cab she smiled at him. "Drive me home, Officer West."

One side of his mouth lifting in a cocky grin, he winked at her. "Yes, ma'am."

Dean drove north then hopped on the interstate to take her home. Once they were cruising at a good speed he reached out to tangle his fingers with hers. Once again, Rachel's heart leapt in her chest and she shook her head, unable to believe how much her normally calm, steady body reacted to his.

Dean had caught the slight movement. "What's wrong?"

She sighed in the darkness, wondering how much to tell him. Everything, if she planned on having a future with him. "I'm just amazed at the reaction you provoke in me."

"Good, I hope," he told her around a toothy grin.

Rachel laughed. "Excellent, actually. I'm not normally the touchy, feely type but you make me not mind it."

His attention had returned to the road, but he shot her a considering look. "Maybe you just haven't been touched and felt the right way?"

"Perhaps," she agreed. "Maybe you can remedy that?"

Dean's eyes widened and they jerked back to hers. He stared at her a long moment before focusing back on the road. His right hand tightened on hers and he didn't release her all the way back to her building.

The curtains twitched next door. Rachel knew Mrs. Lightner would be jotting down in her journal that Rachel had been dropped off by a big, strapping man but that man had stayed hours longer than was proper for an unmarried couple.

Rachel led Dean into her home, helicopters doing aerial maneuvers in her stomach. As she started to lead him to her bedroom, Dean slowed her in the hallway.

"Rachel, I won't hold you to this. I don't want to rush you into anything."

"You're not rushing me into anything," she told him firmly.

Dean's expression turned cautious. "I don't want to rush *us* into anything then. Yes, I'm attracted to you like crazy, I've had a boner damn near since I met you, but I would rather take my time and do this right than rush into something that could possibly ruin the relationship. I'm in this for the long haul, sweetheart."

Those damn helicopters bottomed out in her stomach. She hadn't dared hope he would even say something like that.

CHAPTER EIGHT

T HE FACT THAT he was willing to wait with no recrimina-
tions, no hesitation, confirmed what she already knew in her
heart and mind. Dean West was an incredible man.

Her hand tightened on his. "I am too. But I want to enjoy
this journey as much as I possibly can. As long as you don't
mind me moving a little stiffly, I would like to explore the
physical side of this relationship."

Those normally joyful eyes looked at her with mild reproach.
"As long as you realize that this won't just be a physical
relationship. I want more from you than that, Rachel."

Rachel nodded, hoping he couldn't see the devastation in her
eyes. She'd never expected to find anything even resembling love
and now he was almost offering it on a plate. Daring, she looked
up at him with that hope in her eyes. "And I'm willing to give
you damn near anything you want, Dean."

That heart-flipping smile of his spread across his face as he
leaned down to cover her mouth with his own. Rachel opened to
him, both physically and emotionally.

Dean seemed to sense her new openness. He nibbled at her
lips as he pulled her body close. Rachel gasped as his chest
brushed against hers, back and forth, as if he were deliberately
teasing her. But he wouldn't do that, would he?

Arching her hips, she rubbed against the erection behind his jeans. Groaning, Dean pushed her back against the wall, rocking into the cradle of her hips. His mouth took on a new fervency, fitting to hers completely, his tongue gliding against hers. A wave of arousal ran down the center of her body to her clit and it was almost *too* much. She didn't remember feeling this way with the other men she'd been with and it was a little disconcerting.

Not so disconcerting that she wanted to stop, though.

Rachel ran her hands across the expanse of his abdomen. Muscles flexed beneath her touch, taut and rippled. Her fingers sought for a way inside to his skin. Dean helped her by ripping the shirt over his head and tossing it away to land in a heap against the hallway wall.

Rachel lost her breath as she looked at the beauty in front of her. Broad and massively muscled, lean hipped, Dean looked like the ideal man to her. His touch was incredibly gentle as he burrowed his own hands under her shirt to rest against her skin. Rachel jerked, unused to feeling a man's hand there, but quickly decided she liked it.

"Can we move to my bedroom?" she whispered.

Dean nodded but didn't want to let her go, she could tell. Turning in his hold, she kept his hands on her as she led him to the room.

Rachel was not an interior designer, but of all the rooms in the house she liked to think this one probably gave the most insight into her personality. Though she'd only worn a few shades of military throughout her career, she loved bold colors, quirky objects and things that didn't necessarily go together. The bedroom walls were painted deep blue and decorated with a few pieces of art she'd picked up from around the world, not very expensive things but *expressive*. There were pictures of a herd of elephants in a fog-laden field, a craggy mountain landscape with a single climber and her favorite, a view of the cloud tops from above. It reminded her of flying.

Dean glanced around the room with interest but he didn't let it distract him from his goal. Rachel was nudged into the room, his erection cradled by her butt cheeks. Even before they undressed she could tell they were going to fit well.

Dean ran his thumbs under the elastic of her bra. Rachel stilled, barely daring to breathe. When his hands abruptly left she tried not to be disappointed but he only moved to unfasten her bra. It couldn't go anywhere because it was still under her shirt, but it was now loose enough that he could cup her breasts in his hands. Rachel gasped, hard, at the abrupt feeling of his broad palms cupping her, and her body responded with a flood of moisture down low. "Oh," she moaned.

Dean caressed the weight of her, then his thumbs and forefingers moved to her nipples. Rachel felt like she'd been hit with an electric charge, but he calmed her with kisses against her temple. "If it's too much, let me know."

She nodded because there was no way she could speak right then. Devastating hunger rocked her body and she wanted more, she just wasn't sure how to articulate it. When his hands drifted away from her breasts to her sides and lifted her shirt away, her enjoyment abruptly chilled. Her scars were not pretty at the best of times and she hated that she couldn't see his face.

"Oh, Rachel," he sighed.

Then the most incredible thing happened. He began to drop kisses along the length of her spine. Goose bumps pebbled her flesh from his touch. "Are you sure they don't bother you? I can wear a T-shirt if I need to."

Her breath stalled in her lungs until he moved his head into her line of vision. "And why would I want you to do that?"

She shrugged, a little uncomfortable with the probing look.

"Nobody's seen them so I didn't know if they would freak you out or anything," she muttered lamely.

He moved even more in front of her. "What do you mean no one has seen these?"

God, did she really want to tell him? Not really, but she felt like she needed to. "No one other than medical personnel, that is. I haven't been with anyone since I was injured."

She could hear the ticking of the tiny travel alarm clock on her bedside table, and the slow crumbling of her heart as the time stretched out interminably.

When he moved in to kiss her, Rachel was surprised.

"I'm honored to be the only lover you've ever exposed your injury to, Rachel. Thank you."

Those fucking tears were back and she didn't know what to do with the battering emotions rocketing around inside her. Dean kissed her thoroughly, wiped her eyes then moved back around her. He kissed and accepted every inch of her incision scar in a way that she never expected any man would do.

Hell, maybe it was just a bigger deal to her and he was placating her for sex. As soon as she had the thought, though, she knew she had inadvertently cheapened what they were doing. Dean would never do that and she trusted herself enough to know what she was doing.

When he tugged at the button on her jeans, she was more than happy to help him, shrugging her bra away in the process. Rachel had a process for getting her panties down without bending over very much but Dean took care of that for her, kneeling in front of her with no hesitation. He tugged the lacy pink panties down her legs, sighing as he revealed the moist juncture of her thighs. Nudging her back against the mattress, she rocked onto her back, hands over her head. Dean parted her thighs and leaned between them. Before Rachel had a chance to say anything, he'd buried his mouth against her.

Incredible euphoria stole her breath as he touched her, tongued her, in a place no one ever had before. The hours of arousal watching him, listening to him, smelling him, avalanched over her. With just a couple of strokes from his talented tongue, Dean gave her more pleasure than she'd ever felt in her life.

Rachel screamed, then slammed a hand against her mouth, some inner sense of caution warning her that Mrs. Lightner would call the cops if she thought she was in trouble.

Dean pulled away from her quivering flesh, giving her a grin, and stood up to remove his clothes. Rachel watched dazedly as he shucked everything to the floor, then ripped open a condom to sheathe his extraordinary erection. Rachel had a moment of worry as she caught sight of his incredible body, muscles delineated after many hundreds of hours in gyms. The man could probably bench press a car, but he used incredible care as he settled between her thighs. "Should I let you ride me," he asked.

Rachel gave the question serious thought. "No, I want you inside me just like this. If I'm uncomfortable, I'll let you know."

He needed no further encouragement. Using one hand to guide the head of his cock inside her, he used the other to brace his body over top of her. Rachel lifted her thighs to rest outside his lean hips and she felt the stretch in her back and hips, but no pain.

Dean slid inside her slowly, carefully, as if afraid she were made of glass. "You're not hurting me, Dean. I promise."

Nuzzling his lips into her ear, he sighed. "Okay. Good. I'm just savoring the feel of you. I want to remember everything about our first time together."

She choked out a laugh, her heart shuddering all over again. He knew exactly what to say to her to make her emotions go haywire.

Dean sighed as he reached the edge of her cervix, as deep inside her as he could get. Rachel pulsed around him, still recovering from her initial orgasm. Another quivered deep in her body as he began to move. That nebulous feeling began to build again. "Oh, Dean, you feel so damn good."

He bowed his head and kissed her, nibbling softly at her lips, then up her cheeks to her temple. When he reached the bruise at her hairline he skimmed a gentle kiss there as well. "You do too, sweetheart. You fit me as if we were made for each other."

They did. Hip to hip, chest to ribs, he was just big enough that she would curl perfectly beneath his chin.

After the sex.

He seemed to realize there was more fun to be had because he started flexing his hips into her, then retreating. The long glide of his dick over her sensitive tissues made her frantic to reach that next pinnacle. She clutched at his ass, trying to bring him ever closer.

Dean's movements took on a determination that she could feel to the depths of her being. He planned on making her come again, she could tell, because he was kissing her mouth, then plumping her breasts with one hand. Dean's pleasure soon began to drive the bus, though. She could tell by the way he had begun to shudder, his hips shoving convulsively as if he were unable to curb their movements.

Then he lifted up onto his arms and looked down at her, his stunning eyes half-lidded, hips surging, face slack with pleasure, and she watched and felt him orgasm. His face turned fierce with gratification. The pumping of his hips reached a frenzy, then dramatically slowed as he arched into her.

Rachel thrilled at the look on his face, the enjoyment he was taking from her body. And that satisfaction stoked her own fire and pushed her over the edge. It was as if she had needed him to find release so that she could find her own. The room around them faded away as her world went supernova.

DEAN KNEW HE had to move. He needed to dispose of the condom and they needed to get situated on the bed a little better. Rallying his strength, he pushed up on quivering arms. Rachel stared up at him, a fuzzy, warm, and maybe even loving expression on her face. Her hands tightened on his shoulders as if she was reluctant to release him. Leaning down he kissed her plump lips, unwilling to break the connection they had. "Are you okay? I know I kind of lost control there at the end."

She blinked at him, brows pulling together. "You can lose control like that anytime. My neck is completely fine. You didn't hurt me at all."

Dean grinned, replete, as he began to pull out of her. Even that felt incredible. He sighed as he pushed himself up from her, then he had to pause to etch the way she looked in his memory. Her hair was rumpled but it told him exactly how much he'd pleasured her. Her caramel colored eyes were slumberous and the smile on her lips told him she was as replete as he was. But her spanking hot body drew his gaze.

Rachel drew her thighs together and laid them to the side, creating an elegant curve to her lean frame, one hard-nippled breast pointed toward the ceiling. There were certain things guys just didn't do, especially right after sex. Dropping to the floor in front of her and telling her that he'd just had the best orgasm ever, hands down, would not impress her with his manliness... but that's exactly what he wanted to do.

Instead, he turned for the bathroom to dispose of the condom.

When he returned a few minutes later her eyes had drifted shut. Crawling onto the mattress behind her, he pulled her into the curve of his body, one arm going under her head and the other across her hips.

"Mm," she sighed.

Dean took a deep breath, emotion damn near choking him. "You are incredible, Rachel. I'm sorry you crashed but I'm so thankful I've met you. My heart is fuller than it's ever been. Now that I have you, I don't think I can ever let you go."

Her breath stalled in her chest for a moment, then eased out of her. Her body relaxed against his. "*That* is my secret wish," she whispered, and he felt tears drip onto his arm. His own eyes blurring, he pulled her tighter against his heart, vowing to be more than she'd ever hoped for.

CHAPTER NINE

I T WAS VERY strange waking the next morning. There seemed to be a heater behind her. A very large, lightly snoring heater.

Rachel needed to pee. It had to be about six a.m. Even years after leaving the military, she still got up at the same time every morning. She glanced toward the nightstand but her vision was obscured by a big arm. Well, there was no help for it. She had to go.

Wriggling and pushing, she managed to get Dean's heavy arm away from her shoulders. She was laying on his other arm. As quietly as she could she maneuvered her way out of the cocoon of her bed and padded to the bathroom.

When she returned, there was just enough light to see Dean's sleepy face, smiling softly at her. He propped himself up on an elbow and watched her enter the room.

Rachel hadn't thought he'd be awake yet, so she hadn't bothered covering herself. Now she wished she had. When she reached for a t-shirt lying on the dresser, he sat up. "Please don't. Just let me look at you."

She was so thankful for the weak light coming in the bedroom window. It gave her some semblance of coverage. Dean seemed to see everything, though.

Without being self-conscious of his own stunning nudity he

left the bed and crossed the room to her. Rachel held perfectly still, though her heart threatened to pound out of her chest. When he reached her, Dean stopped inches away. "You look like a seductress. Shadows and light playing across your skin." He stroked the very tip of her nipple. "Are you trying to wake me up?"

Rachel glanced down the length of their bodies. "I think you already woke up," she said softly, leaning into his hardness.

Dean chuckled and wrapped his arms around her back, backing her carefully against the edge of the bed. "Maybe..." he drawled as he lowered her to the mattress and rolled on the condom that he'd palmed from the bedside table.

Rachel shivered in the cool of the room. Or was it him making her shiver? Probably both. As he shifted his big body over hers and he became all she could see and feel and smell, she decided it was definitely Dean that made her body react like this.

When he pressed into her ready heat, Rachel moaned, unable to keep her body from tightening around him. And as he rocked into her, lean hips surging beneath her hands, she allowed herself to languish in the decadent nature of his arousal. He was massive in body and heart. Though she had some experience, she'd never warmed physically or emotionally to another man like she had with Dean. It was overwhelming, and just a little scary.

Already, she could tell that her heart was irretrievably wrecked.

Dean reached down, cupping her thighs and lifting her knees. Arching above her he looked down at her in the dim light. "Are you okay?"

Rachel nodded, panting. "Oh, yes. That feels incredible," she sighed.

Dean seemed to think so as well because his movements began to speed up. His rhythm lost a little of its perfection, being overwhelmed by excitement. Rachel arched her hips, needing contact a little to the right. *Oh, yes, right there.* Her breath caught in her throat as the welling heat of her orgasm rolled over her. "Oh, *Dean*," she cried out. Then she couldn't say anything else.

Keeping the rhythm, he waited until her euphoria had eased before pulling out of her. Rachel blinked up at him in surprise, but he grinned at her. "Trust me."

His broad hands carefully gripped her hips and turned her over, then he pulled her up onto her knees. Rachel would have been embarrassed if she could have seen herself, but the eroticism of the position supplanted her embarrassment. She felt Dean behind her, looking at her.

"Are you okay, sweetheart?"

Rachel nodded immediately. "I am. Just didn't expect this."

Dean ran a hand from her shoulders to her ass, pausing to draw a circle on the skin of her butt cheek. "You have a beautiful shape. I've thought about it way too much."

Rachel snorted. "Really?"

Without answer he wedged his hips tight against her, his cock nestled between them. He rocked them up, spreading the moisture from her release. Rachel sighed as he shifted, the flared head of his dick slipping into her entrance.

Dean felt even harder in this position. More potent. Rachel braced her arms against the mattress, then one against the brown padded headboard for extra leverage. Oh, hell... he was stroking over her G-spot with every stroke. Rachel arched, shifting her hips slightly so that he was in a better groove. Yeah, he'd probably flipped her over for him, but she planned to enjoy the position as well.

Behind her, Dean began huffing out breaths in time to his pumping. Rachel wiggled her ass, teasing him, until he clamped his heavy hands around her hips to hold her still. "I can't look at you like this very long without coming. You have such a beautiful ass."

Rachel laughed, then gasped as he reached forward to cup her breasts in his hands. The bed creaked as he plunged into her, but Rachel could only arch back into him because he felt so good. As he surged deeper than he had before she cried out, making him pause. "No, it's all good. Keep going, damn it!"

Dean picked up the rhythm and it began to change. The tension in his body leached into hers and Rachel felt her orgasm dancing just out of reach. Dean seemed to sense it because he managed to reach a hand down around to between her thighs. One thick finger glided between her soaked folds to lightly tap her clit. Rachel cried out and tightened around him. That was all it took for them both to plunge over the cliff.

Dean growled something against her but she couldn't tell what. She was too busy trying to stay up on her arms as his full weight rested on her hips and his orgasm crashed over him.

Rachel moaned as the aftershocks consumed her. Dean's head rested against the back of her own for a moment before he pulled away. Her body tried to keep him close but it didn't work.

They both collapsed to the bed, sweaty but replete. Rachel couldn't remember ever feeling so boneless yet satisfied. Her body thrummed with pleasure and her stomach twitched with aftershocks. The morning had lightened enough that when she looked at Dean, she could see the satisfied grin on his face.

"You rock my world, woman."

Rachel laughed, curling on her side to face him. "You're not bad yourself, Officer West."

And it was so very true. If she could have anyone to fall in love with, Dean was an excellent choice. They just *fit*.

They spent a lazy morning showering and dressing, then

Dean made them an easy scrambled egg breakfast. Rachel offered to do it but he waved her away. "Let me pamper you."

That phrase kind of sat her right back down on her ass. Nobody had ever pampered her. Or if they tried she'd gone glacial on them. As she watched Dean move through her kitchen doing a job she had no desire to do anyway, she decided that she could accept a little pampering. It certainly wouldn't kill her.

"I need to go to the range at some point today," he told her, stirring the eggs. "We have qualifications next week. Would you like to join me?"

Rachel hesitated. Though she was mostly recovered from the crash, the thought of listening to that many guns going off in such close proximity to her wasn't all that appealing today. And if she had a reaction to the noise, she'd rather it not be in front of Dean. "Not today, but thank you for asking. Maybe I can go with you next time."

Dean smiled but he looked a little disappointed too. He left after he helped her clean up their dishes and as she watched his truck pull out of her driveway, Rachel was both a little sad and kind of relieved that he was leaving. It had been a long time since she'd been in a relationship and the constant companionship over the past day had been a little difficult to get used to.

She probably should have told him that range firing like that sometimes took her back to not so nice times, but the right moment to explain had escaped her.

Maybe she just felt a little squeamish about last night. He'd basically told her he wasn't going anywhere and she wasn't sure how to react to that. She'd taken care of herself for so many years. Did she want to be dependent on another person? Not necessarily.

Rachel picked up the apartment a little and tried to watch the news, but it didn't keep her interest. She decided to drive into

work. It was Saturday afternoon, but she knew somebody would be there. Maybe she could get in a light workout.

DEAN PRACTICED WITH his service weapon and grabbed more ammo for later. As he was walking to the counter to check out he noticed a jewelry display. Not something he'd ever noticed before. Curious, he crossed to see what might draw a woman in a gun store.

It was bullets. Actually, just the cap of bullets, where the caliber was imprinted into the metal. The primer at the center had been replaced with a small gemstone. Dean laughed as he looked at the variety of key chains, necklaces and earrings. Would Rachel be into something like this?

The longer he looked at the display the more he liked them. His gaze settled on a set of earrings with 9mm caps and diamond-like cubic zirconia in the center.

Or... there was another pair with real diamonds in them.

Damn. He'd been with the woman for a couple of days and was already buying her jewelry. She had him so bowled over ... but he felt more centered and sure than ever before in his life.

Without fighting with himself too much, he went with the real diamonds. They weren't huge, so it wasn't going to break the bank, but they were definitely more expensive than the CZ.

"Those are nice," the salesman told him. "I bought my wife a pair this past Christmas and it's all she wears. Where's the gun?"

Dean looked at him. "I'm sorry?"

The older man laughed. "Well, usually the guys are buying earrings to balance out the money they spent on the gun they weren't supposed to buy."

Dean laughed and shook his head as he signed the receipt. "I get you now, but no, no gun this time." He paused in thought. "Maybe I should have gotten her a gun."

The old man laughed out loud. "That's not a bad idea. More men are doing that for their wives nowadays."

Dean didn't correct him on the wife part. Actually, it kind of made him happy that the guy had said it. No, Rachel wasn't his wife yet, but he liked trying it on for size.

The old guy dropped the jewelry box into a bag decorated with the store's name. "Good luck!"

Dean walked out of the store feeling like something big was about to happen. When should he give them to her? Should it be a big deal or kind of off-hand, in case she spooked? Maybe he should talk to Killian about it.

Realistically, he knew theirs was a young relationship. But it felt as though he had known her much longer than mere days. He'd been in relationships with other women, but none of them had made him feel this way. Maybe he would just take his time and see what developed.

CHAPTER TEN

S HANNON LOOKED UP from the phone in her hand when Rachel unlocked the door to the office and walked in. John's fiancé grinned. "Hey, Rachel. How are you feeling?"

She'd been asked that so many times in the past few days it had obliterated her last nerve, but it seemed different coming from Shannon. "I'm actually not too bad. Once I get these itchy stitches out I'll be as good as new."

Shannon looked at her forearm with an understanding nod. "John would have pulled them out by now if he were the one injured."

Rachel sighed. "Yeah, I probably would have too, but there's one little section deeper than the rest. I'll let the stitches do their job. Then I'll yank them."

Laughing, Shannon circled the desk to plop down into her chair, hand going to her barely-there belly. "Are you just here to visit or work?"

Rachel shrugged. "Whatever. Who's here?"

"No one right now. It's pretty dead today. Even Duncan went home this weekend."

Damn, Rachel thought. The world must be ending. That kind of derailed her plan.

"Is there anything I can help you with?"

Rachel looked at the small, pretty woman and took her courage in hand. "Are you busy?"

Shannon blinked and glanced down at the blotter, then back up. "No, not really. A client came in this morning to drop off a check but I'm pretty much free now. I was just catching up on some tax stuff. Why?"

Rachel shifted on her feet, a little uncomfortable. "Were you serious when you offered to go shopping with me?"

Excitement lightened Shannon's pretty hazel eyes. "Of course I was. Let me put a few things away and we can lock up on our way out."

Rachel wondered what she'd let herself in for. Shannon was really nice, but would she be able to spend hours with her?

It turned out that she could. John's fiancé was truly a remarkable woman, but Rachel had kind of already known that. Hell, the woman damn near had to be a saint to be able to put up with Palmer's nasty disposition.

As they went from store to store, though, at the Northfield Stapleton Mall, Rachel realized how much feminine information was packed into Shannon's head. Yes, a lot of it was basic and usable for most women, but Rachel doubted she would use it very often. They went to a high-end department store and received tips on make-up. Though she cringed at the ridiculous prices, Rachel bought a couple of items like some foundation and eye shadow that even she had to admit looked good on her and made her eyes seem luminous.

Over her objections, Shannon escorted her to a clothing store with gear that seemed to be a little young for her. She cringed at some of the displays.

"Don't you like dresses?"

Rachel frowned. "No. No dresses. Definitely not my cup of tea."

"But are they *his* cup of tea?"

Did Dean like dresses? With a sigh she conceded he probably did. Most men did, right? "Yeah, maybe."

Shannon pulled a couple of dresses from the racks that weren't completely hideous, so Rachel stepped into the changing room to try them on. On the first one, the top was definitely skimpier than what she was used to and the bottom felt completely exposed! She had to check the mirror several times to make sure that the fabric wasn't tucked into her panties or something. It felt too drafty.

Shannon's eyes widened when Rachel stepped out and she moved forward to tug at a couple of folds. "Dude, you look hot in this," she hissed. "With your body you can pull off just about anything you put on."

Rachel wasn't convinced. The biggest drawback was that the scar on her neck was exposed. There were a few other women around but as soon as she became aware of them it felt like they were all looking at her. "I'm not sure I can wear this."

Shannon retrieved a sweater type thing from a nearby rack. "Would this make you more comfortable?"

Rachel swallowed, so appreciative that Shannon seemed to understand her reticence. Shrugging the shoulder cover on, Rachel turned to look at the three-reflection mirror. "Okay, maybe I don't look hideous in this."

Shannon laughed lightly. "I told you, you look *hot!*"

Hot would be stretching it. Better than expected would be more accurate. She turned, looking at as many views as she could. Yes, she had a decent shape. Maybe better than average boobs. Her legs were strong and lean. "What shoes would I wear with this?"

Shannon produced a pair of strappy flat sandals from a nearby shelf. Impressed, Rachel looked at the small woman and wondered how the heck she knew what size Rachel wore in everything. Shannon grinned at her and winked.

Rachel walked out of the store with several new outfits, including the dress and sandals. She had tried everything on and gotten Shannon's approval. And before she knew what was going on, she had told Shannon all about Dean.

"He sounds like a total sweetheart," Shannon had sighed at one point. "It probably doesn't matter what you wear for him."

Rachel agreed. But she still bought the clothes, for herself as much as for him.

After hitting several other stores and taking the bags to the car, they stopped for dinner at a popular eatery known for their ribs.

"I think I can eat an entire pig," Shannon sighed. "I can't believe how hungry I've been the past few weeks. The nausea is finally easing up. Anything is better than that."

Rachel wished she could compare stories with Shannon about babies and pregnancies, but it wasn't actually anything she'd ever considered part of her future. Not until Dean.

"Is Palmer happy?"

They were interrupted by the waiter just then, of course. They gave their order and Rachel sipped at her Diet-Coke as Shannon thought about the question. "I think overall he's happy, but he's worried, too. I mean, handling a baby isn't easy even when you have legs, so he's really going to have to adapt. We're going to have to develop ways for him to take part in the baby's life." She sighed, sipping her water. "I wouldn't change John for anything but there are times I wish there were easier ways for him to do things."

Rachel nodded, totally understanding. Every one of the men she worked with were amazing in spite of the fact that they couldn't live the way they used to. They all had a different reality.

"I think he'll rock being a dad just like he does everything else."

Shannon nodded, a contented smile on her face. "He will and our kids will be amazing." She leaned forward, propping her elbows on the table. "Have you ever thought about having kids?"

Tit for tat. Rachel supposed she needed to be as honest and open as Shannon and answer. "Yes, a little, but there was never anyone to have them with. Dean is the first guy to enter my life who I would even consider having children with...like ever."

And though she hadn't thought about it so specifically like that, she realized her words were true. Dean was a great guy. He would be a fabulous husband and a terrific father.

After dinner the women hiked back to the car and Shannon drove them back to the office, where they'd left Rachel's bike. Shannon was anxious to get back to Palmer and looking worn out, to boot. Rachel leaned forward and gave the woman a tight hug. "Thank you so much for taking me out today and spending my money."

Shannon laughed. "Anytime, hon!"

With a little wave Rachel exited the car and walked to the motorcycle, bags in hand. It was a challenge stowing the bags, but she managed.

When she arrived home she realized how tired she was, too. Who knew shopping was this exhausting? Dropping the bags to the floor she moved into her bedroom, shucking clothes as she went. The hot water of the shower washed away some of her tiredness and relaxed the muscles in her neck. As she dried off, she wondered what Dean was doing just then. She hadn't heard from him all day.

The green light on her cell-phone blinked, indicating she had a message. As she swiped the screen she grinned. Speak of the devil.

Hey, beautiful. Wondering if you had time for a call? Just got off shift.

Rather than typing out a message she dialed his number. Dean answered on the first ring.

"I didn't wake you, did I?"

"No," she said, settling to the mattress. "I just got home, actually. Shannon and I went shopping."

"Shannon?"

"Oh, she's the Office Manager for LNF and the fiancé of one of the partners. Nice lady."

"Ah, okay. I'm glad you had fun."

Rachel reached a corner of her towel up to squeeze the end of her dripping hair. "I did. And I didn't expect to. I guess I didn't expect to get along with her so well but she surprised me with how cool she was."

"Well," he said slowly, "that's good, right?"

"Oh, yes, of course. I don't have a lot of girlfriends here so it was nice."

"What spurred the outing?"

Rachel hesitated, unwilling to tell him she'd gone shopping for dates with him. "Well, actually, we went shopping for clothes."

The silence stretched on his end. "Did you get anything nice?"

Rachel grinned at the interest she heard in his voice, and she thought of the pink and black striped lingerie bag in the hallway. "Well, maybe…"

"You tease," he whispered.

Laughing, she reclined back onto the bed, wondering if it was too late for him to come over. "Well, it's not teasing if there's follow-through, right?"

Again, silence drew out and she wondered if she'd gone too far. "It's teasing if it can't be acted upon for the foreseeable future. I have an early shift tomorrow."

Moaning, she sat up against the headboard. "Okay. I guess I'll be good."

Dean laughed on the other end of the line, a full-throated, deep chuckle. "I guess somebody is feeling better today."

"I am, definitely."

Yes, the stitches still itched like a bitch and a half, but the skin beneath them was healing. She would give them two more days before they got pulled. The contusions around the gash on her face were beginning to yellow out as well. A few more days and it wouldn't even be visible. And today had been the first day she hadn't noticed the bruises on her calf aching with every step. The only thing she had noticed was some tenderness down below. When they'd made love she'd started using muscles that hadn't been used in a long time. Things were a bit sore, but there was a satisfaction in using those muscles again.

"Why don't you come over after your shift? I'll throw to-gether something for dinner." Rachel cringed, wondering what kind of microwave dinners he would eat.

Dean seemed a little surprised too. "Okay," he drawled. "I'll be over after I stop at my apartment and change. Want me to bring a movie or something?"

"Sure. Anything."

The conversation began to dwindle but neither one seemed willing to hang up. Finally, frustrated with all of these too-girly emotions swirling around her, Rachel told him goodnight and hung up the phone.

Just a few minutes later she was sound asleep.

FOR DEAN, EARLY Sunday shift was one of the best to work. Ninety percent of the people in Denver were either sleeping in or attending church. The other ten percent were heading for their favorite hiking trails. It was going to be a beautiful day today and the outdoors were calling. If he weren't working it was where he would be as well.

Because it was so quiet, though, the hours dragged on. He looked for traffic violations but didn't find many. No alarm checks, no welfare checks. Nothing happened until an hour before his shift ended. Then he and another car were dispatched for a hit and run multi-car pile-up. Tapping out a quick message he told Rachel he would be as quick as possible, then ran hot to the scene.

CHAPTER ELEVEN

RACHEL LOOKED AT the message in consternation. Figures. She'd been counting down the hours until she could see him again and their date was delayed. No, it wasn't the fault of the people who crashed, and she would never think such things, but it was still disappointing. Grabbing her iPad she plugged in her headphones. Maybe she could lose herself in music. Or games. Candy Crush Saga had her at a standstill. Maybe if she spent enough money on boosters she could get past the hurdle and move on.

It was three hours later before she heard a knock on her door. Trying to control the excited leap of her heart she crossed the room and swung open the door. Dean stood there, a smile on his face.

Something was off, though, she could tell.

"Come on in," she urged him.

Dean leaned down to press a kiss to her lips before he even stepped over the threshold. Rachel cupped his head in her hands and tried to be what he needed, because there was something off about his kiss as well. She pulled back, concerned. "Are you okay?"

He blinked down at her, his blue eyes dull. Rachel suddenly realized what it was rattling her senses. He looked like the guys she'd flown into Afghanistan time after time, ready to do the job, but emotionally detached. Those men had seen too much in their very young lives and she would remember the look for as long as she lived. If she dared look in the mirror, she would probably see the same expression on her own face.

Dean didn't need sex or food, he needed a non-judgmental ear and a warm shoulder next to his own. Tugging him into the room, Rachel nudged him toward the couch. Dean dropped his nylon uniform bag on the chair then followed her willingly and collapsed onto the cushions. Rachel plopped down beside him, hip-to-hip and shoulder-to-shoulder.

"How was your shift?" she asked, going straight to the issue.

Dean winced and looked away. "It was great for a while. Totally quiet."

"The message said you had a hit and run to deal with?"

He nodded, running his hand through his thick blond hair, making it stick up in spikes. "Yeah. It was bad. One of the worst I've ever dealt with."

"Why was this one so bad?" she asked.

He hesitated for a long time but she didn't push him to answer. Reaching out she curled her fingers into his. His grip tightened until her fingers ached.

"One of the victims was just a little kid. Five years old. So tiny on her little pink bike. I think she was gone almost instantly. Her older brother is in critical condition although he's expected to survive. The car that hit them then veered into oncoming traffic and hit four cars before his vehicle was so damaged it wouldn't move anymore. Then he still wouldn't get out of the car." He gave her a chagrined look. "I actually enjoyed dragging his ass out of the wreckage and onto the pavement. Stupid shit. He was laughing when we took him down. Thought the whole deal was funny."

Damn. Rachel's heart ached at the obvious sorrow in his expression. "Dean," she breathed, "I'm so sorry. Drugs or alcohol?"

"Meth. The car was littered with paraphernalia."

Rachel shook her head in commiseration. She'd heard the same story, or variations of it, many times over the years. There had been a pilot in her squadron that had had a very well hidden cocaine addiction. It wasn't until his own flight team turned him in that anyone knew about it. Luckily, they'd gotten him out of the air before he hurt anyone seriously or crashed and hurt a whole lot of someones.

"You know there is nothing you could have done differently. If it wasn't that guy it would have been someone else plowing into that crowd. You deal with the situation that you find, then you have to move on."

Dean nodded, sighing. "I know. Life is just so precious, though, you know?"

Rachel barked out a laugh. "Yes, I do know how precious it is. Believe me. When my chopper started to go down, I knew it was the end of my life. But I was okay with it, because that was part of why I had signed on. Giving your life for your country is acceptable, right?"

She shook her head, lost in memory. "Then we hit the ground and pain just exploded through my body. But I was still alive. Somebody moaned behind me and I knew I needed to get my ass moving. I had a lot to do. But I couldn't move. That was when I realized maybe I should have died in that crash. I thought I was going to be a cripple for the rest of my life and I would rather be dead."

Dean gripped her hand in his own like a lifeline, without saying anything.

"I passed out and basically didn't wake up for a week. By

then I was in Germany, recovering. None of my guys died that day, but a bunch were pretty beat up. A couple got shipped stateside. I got shipped stateside as well and received a medical release. There was no way I could go back in service." She shrugged as if the changes that took place then had been minor. "You roll with the punches and keep going. This will knock you down for a while, but when you go back out you'll be a sharper cop for it. I know it hurts, but that pain will drive you."

"Why haven't you ever flown again?"

The question came out of nowhere and Rachel sat back against the couch, surprise taking her breath away. "I just don't..." she trailed off, shaking her head.

"This is kind of the same thing, right? I mean, why haven't you flown again?"

Rachel didn't know what to say now that the light was shining directly on her. Was he just trying to shift the attention away from himself? No, knowing Dean he'd already been thinking about this. "I don't know. I think I would be disappointed if I couldn't do it the way I used to. I don't have the same range of motion that I did and that's a big part of flying." She shrugged and made a motion with her hands. "I wouldn't have that adrenaline rush, you know? Flying in, blacked-out, under heavy fire to retrieve forty Marines pinned down in the mountains is a pretty tough act to beat."

Dean inclined his head and leaned back against the couch, wrapping his arm around her shoulders. "Yeah, you may be right."

And he left it at that.

Rachel frowned, curious at the conversation. He'd accepted her statements easily. Maybe too easily. She was confused at what she felt. Did she want him to argue with her? Did she want him to push her to do something she'd kind of been wondering about anyway?

"Well," he said finally. "I think we both realize how tenuous life can be. I have something for you."

She watched as he left the couch and rummaged in the duffel. He brought a smallish paper bag over to her. Intrigued, she reached inside and pulled out a box.

Her heart stilled. It was a midnight blue velvet jewelry box.

For a minute she didn't do anything, just sat on the couch with the box in her hand and her heart suddenly racing. Then common sense moved in, it wasn't square. It wasn't a ring box. At least, she didn't *think* it was.

Blinking to clear her vision, she used her other hand to pop open the lid.

Then, once again, her heart was torn in two. No, it wasn't a ring, which was a complete, and very surprising letdown. But it was a pair of beautiful earrings. She peered at them and flicked the stone with a fingernail, laughing. "What? Are these bullets?"

"Well, I think they used to be. Or at least the rim and primer part."

Rachel blinked, then removed one of the earrings from the velvet covered cardboard. She turned it over in her fingers, looking at the workmanship. "These are beautiful. I've never seen anything like them."

Reaching up she removed the plain silver studs she wore, placing them on the coffee-table in front of her. Then she replaced the studs with the bullet earrings. She shook her head, laughing, then stood to cross to him. "These are ridiculous and beautiful and silly, but I love them. Thank you very much."

Rachel had planned to give him a light peck, playful, but emotion choked her. Wrapping her arms around his neck she leaned into him. "Nobody's ever gotten me anything like them before. Thank you."

Dean wrapped her up tight and swayed with her a little. "I had to laugh at the guy at the gun store. He thought I was buying them to get me out of the doghouse for buying a gun."

Rachel laughed, enjoying the irony. She'd have been happy with a gun, too. "That is funny," she told him, enjoying having his arms wrapped around her.

DEAN RELISHED HOLDING Rachel in his arms, but something niggled at him. It had been disappointment he'd seen in her eyes when she'd opened the box. He guessed if he was a woman who had been handed a jewelry box, he'd have wanted it to be something different as well. But it seemed too soon for an engagement ring. Or any kind of ring for that matter.

He loved that she was thinking about marriage, whether she realized it or not. Rachel seemed to be one of those types that would fight and fight and fight until they finally did a one-eighty. It was like the flying thing.

Dean had a feeling that Rachel would love to fly again, but she didn't want to admit it until she absolutely had to, especially to herself. So there was no sense in pushing her before she was ready.

If he had anything to say about it she *would* fly again.

They settled into a quiet evening at home. Thoughts of the little girl on the bicycle and a family grieving popped up occasionally, but he would glance at Rachel fingering her earrings and things would fall back into perspective. This was what was important. He would file the details of the day into his heart and mind and be a better cop when he went back to work.

That night they crawled into bed and he just held her for a long time. Dean didn't consider himself a weepy kind of guy, but he definitely felt he could be emotional with her if he needed to.

There was no need to pretend that he wasn't affected by what had happened. He'd seen the glimmer of tears in her eyes as well. His kick-ass Marine had a soft spot.

So, he held her against him, lightly rubbing his hand up the skin of her arm. He'd found that she loved to be lightly stroked this way, along her sides and across her back. It was no hardship to him; he loved touching her.

But that, of course, led to other things. And as he loved her into the night, he wondered if she was as affected by him as he was by her.

CHAPTER TWELVE

R ACHEL DIDN'T SEE Dean for a couple of days, though they texted fairly often. He sent her jokes about the military and she sent him fat cop jokes. It was all in good fun. Then he mixed in sexy jokes about stripping her out of her BDUs and shirt to check out her lingerie and it all went to hell.

As she headed in to work out before her shift, she wondered if he were getting ready for work as well. Their day shift hours were similar, but they lived too far apart to work out together. Maybe someday. Or maybe they needed to shift their workout times completely so that they could be together.

Rachel set her phone aside as she headed into the rec room to the free weights. It wasn't until about halfway through her workout that she heard a strange sound. What was that?

Her phone giggled. Rachel wiped off her hands and snatched up her device, paging through her notifications. She looked around at the men in the room. "Okay, you jackasses, who did it?"

As soon as she said the words Chad laughed. She should have known. "What did you do to my phone?"

A message notification lit her screen and it giggled. Rachel fought not to smile. "You've been hanging out with your little girl too much. You have Minions on the brain."

Chad laughed. "I think you're right."

Every time she received a text message a Minion giggled. John had glowered at the disruption to his workout, but even his hard mouth twitched when she got an alert.

Rachel punched Chad in the arm. "You ass."

Chad grinned at her. "Darlin', I just wanted you to smile more. Something's got you down. That cop you've been seeing better be taking good care of you."

That kind of rocked her back on her heels. Was she down?

Rachel looked around the workout room. It was a busy day. At least four of the guys were working out. Chad had just gotten off the treadmill from his fifty-mile run or whatever. Seemed like he ran forever, that damn blade on his left leg flashing. She wasn't sure when he'd even messed with her phone. Oh, yeah, she'd gone to the bathroom at one point. That's right. He'd probably snatched it up then.

Palmer sat on the curl bench, biceps bulging as he worked the weights. Gabe Carter, the new SEAL they'd hired, worked free weights a few feet away from her. He was quiet and a little sad but definitely seemed competent and had even spotted her a couple of times.

All of them had an ease to their expressions that she was sure hers did not. Why was she so on edge?

A Minion giggled and she looked down at her phone. *Can we get together tonight?*

Immediately she could feel her expression change. She swiped the sweat from her hands and tapped out *yes, definitely!*

As soon as they had plans to get together, some tension in her eased. Was it that simple? She'd been in a grumpy mood because she hadn't seen Dean for two days? Maybe because they hadn't made love in two days. She needed that connection again.

Sighing, she powered off the phone and turned back to her

weights, suddenly feeling a lot more positive about the day. And night.

DEAN HAD BARELY finished knocking on the door before Rachel pulled it open. Immediately his eyes drifted down her shape, backlit by the living room lamps. Wait. Holy ... What the hell was she wearing?

Stepping inside he looked down at her. Subtle make-up high-lighted her eyes, making them seem bigger and clearer. And she was wearing a freaking dress. Something long and gorgeous and split on the side so that he could see her thigh. Immediately, a bolt of arousal arrowed down through him, waking up all parts of his previously tired body.

Before she could move out of the way, he leaned down to kiss her glossed lips. "You look stunning."

Though it was dim in the hallway he thought his no-nonsense Marine might have blushed. She waved a hand and pulled him inside. "Whatever."

She started to pull away but he put a hand on her elbow. "No, you are. You are beautiful. Maybe not in the conventional sense, but it's all in the eye of the beholder, right? I paid you a compliment because you are absolutely stunning to me. You need to take it nicely and believe what I say."

Damn, he wished there was more light in here. Now he thought he saw tears glinting in her eyes.

"Okay," she whispered. "Thank you."

When she turned he allowed her to lead him into the room. There was quite a spread on the dining room table; two different kinds of pizza and a big bowl of salad.

Dean looked at her in consternation. "How do you stay so damn fit? Do you eat fast food all the time?"

Rachel propped her hands on her hips and he forgot what they were talking about. She looked gorgeous in her flowing green dress. The damn thing cupped her yummy breasts, swept in at her tight waist and flared out, draping gently round her hips. It was the most feminine thing he'd ever seen her wear.

"...and why are you staring at me like that? Have you heard anything I've said?"

Dean blinked and stepped close, tilting her chin up with his finger. "No, I haven't. I've been too busy drooling. Is this one of the things you bought the other day?" he motioned down to her dress.

"Y-yes." Then she smiled. "And a few other things."

Arousal hardened him even more as his eyes drifted down. "Oh, really? Like what?"

"Well, I bought some casual outfits. You know, something other than BDUs and t-shirts."

He leaned into her, brushing his lips against her temple. "What else?"

"Well, I got some sandals to go with the dresses. I feel very naked with them on though."

Dean chuckled. She probably did feel naked. He'd only ever seen her in boots.

"What else?" he whispered.

"Well, Shannon talked me into going to Victoria's Secret, and I have to admit, there were some very... wow... um, kinda, um, *wild* things in there. I might have bought something..."

His erection pushed at the zipper of his pants. Holy hell, she was going to kill him. Just the thought of lingerie on her already fabulous body was the stuff of dreams. "What did you buy?" he demanded in a harsh, strangled, whisper.

Without answering him, Rachel nudged him backwards until he dropped to the couch cushions. "Wait here," she ordered.

She reached behind him to swing the drapes closed on the front windows, then she padded barefoot into the dim hallway.

Dean wrapped his hand around his dick, debating whether or not to strip down. No, he would let her do that. She could come out wearing a potato sack and he would still think her the loveliest thing, the most beautiful woman on the planet. She was leery of his compliments, though. He would have to remedy that. Or just beat her down with repetition. He would *make* her believe she was beautiful.

There was a thump in the hallway and he looked up in time to see her enter the room.

His heart melted, but he almost came in his pants. Rachel stood uncertainly in the living room doorway, unsure where to put her hands. And he could understand her problem.

Rachel wore a, well, he guessed it was a negligee. He wasn't really sure exactly what it was called. A froth of off-white satin fell to mid-thigh. See-through lace held her breasts but certainly didn't hide them. Actually, the pattern of the lace itself seemed to highlight her dark nipples.

Her dark blond hair was down around her face and he couldn't see her expression, which worried him. Then she cocked a hip provocatively and started to walk toward him.

"So," her voice was whisper soft and nervous. "What do you think?"

Dean barked out a laugh, surprised that he could actually speak. "I think I could come in my pants in about three seconds."

His arms were spread along the back of the couch, clutching the cushions and his breathing had deepened. If she didn't come over here soon, he was going to have to go after her.

Rachel seemed to understand that he was about at the end of his rope. Moving into the room, her tan legs looking miles long, she made her way to him.

Dean could see her face now and he hoped the look in her eyes meant what he thought it did. She went to her knees in front of him and wedged in between them, leaning into him as she started to unbutton his shirt. Dean cupped her shoulders in his hands, then ran a finger along the length of her clavicle and down her chest. He could feel the heavy beat of her heart beneath his touch. He wasn't the only one affected.

When she reached his waistband, Rachel didn't even hesitate. She unbuckled his pants, pulled apart the zipper then leaned back and gripped the fabric at his hips. Understanding what she wanted he lifted up enough that she could jerk his pants and underwear down beneath his ass. His cock sprang free, no worse for the rough handling. Dean found it incredibly exciting that she was so focused and driven. The two days apart had apparently been as hard for her as it had been for him. With a saucy grin, she lowered her head to drop a line of kisses down his belly to his groin.

Warm, wet heat enveloped the head of his cock and he was right back on the edge of climax. Rachel had a talented tongue and seemed to know how close he was. Or maybe it was the convulsive grip he had on her arms telling her how close he was.

One of Rachel's strong hands slid beneath the couch cushion to grip his ass while the other held the base of his cock for her mouth to explore.

Dean was shocked at how confidently, how completely, she held his pleasure in her hands. She took him to the very edge of climax, then moved her mouth to kiss other areas, letting him regain control. It was during one of these times that he wrested control from her.

With a strong grip beneath her shoulders he lifted her up into his arms.

"I wanted to finish you that way," she complained.

"Another time," he growled. "It's my turn to explore."

He reclined her over his lap, his erection nestled beneath her ass. When she settled and flexed one of her legs he got a flash of dark curls at the juncture of her thighs as the fabric rode high. Immediately, he was right on the edge of climax again. She wasn't wearing any panties.

Holding her shoulders with his left arm, he used his right to explore. Tracing a finger up the length of her thigh, he ran it beneath the edge of the beautiful negligee. Yes, she was completely bare. Her outer curls were soaked with arousal and he played there for a moment, praying that he could hold off his own pleasure long enough for her to come first.

She didn't want to just lay back and let him do everything, though. With a twist she cupped the back of his head and brought him closer until their mouths connected. Dean sank into her sweetness, wondering how the hell he'd been lucky enough to find her. Rachel moaned, her tongue gliding against his.

Dean started to caress her outer curls till his finger slipped into her moisture and into the heat of her body. Her clit pulsed beneath his thumb as he circled it, then again, and again. Rachel ripped her mouth away, gasping as he circled faster and faster. It was when he began to tap that she let out a muffled scream and came.

Dean clutched her to him, fondling her lightly to prolong her pleasure, but within just a few seconds she pushed away from him and stood. Then, before he had a chance to say anything, she spread her thighs and straddled his lap. Unerringly, his cock slid deep within her. They both cried out and stilled. Rachel's inner muscles quivered around his length and he knew that as soon as she started to move he would be done.

As if she heard his thoughts she sat deep into his lap, her

long elegant thighs spread around them, and she started to grind. Her hands were clasped on his shoulders and neck, so he was free to cup her swollen breasts in his palms. The lace was also flexible enough that he could lift her breasts free of the cups. Dean shook his head at the sultry, sexy picture they made.

Her hips started a mind-numbing swivel and all coherent thought left his mind. Three times she moved like that, her eyes closed and head lolled back, and he was a goner. The orgasm that he'd been holding at bay rocketed up through his cock unlike anything he'd ever felt before, and he let the pleasure burn through his body. At some point he gripped her hips to hold her close as she convulsed with her own orgasm. Eventually she melted against him, tucking into his chest, and they just basked in the lingering pleasure.

Dean cradled Rachel to him and was overcome with an emotion so profound he'd never felt it before. It curled in around his heart as surely as she was curled in his lap. It was humbling and heartening and he wanted it to last forever.

TEARS BURNED IN Rachel's eyes, but she refused to let them fall. What they had done was stunning but she refused to be a blubbering mess around Dean. Instead, breathing steadily to calm her heart, she stroked her hand up his neck to cup the back of his head. Then she kissed him, trying to tell him more than any words could how much she appreciated him and enjoyed being with him. He rocked her world. Period.

Her balance swam as he pushed to his feet, with her still cradled in his arms. She felt him kick his pants away, his chest muscles bulging as he balanced them. Rachel was not a small woman by any means, but Dean did not seem to even notice her weight.

Angling to the side to clear the doorway, he swept into her bedroom, then her master bath. There he set her on her feet.

Rachel glanced up into the mirror and chuckled softly. They both looked royally fucked—no lie. Dean stepped behind her, grinning, and cupped her lace-covered breasts. "You can welcome me home like that anytime, sweetheart." Then he frowned. "Although we didn't use anything to prevent a pregnancy."

She smiled, loving the concern she saw in his eyes. "As long as you're clean, it's not an issue. I have a long-term IUD in."

His glorious eyes flared with excitement. "I'm completely clean and you have no idea how happy that makes me. Thank you, Rachel."

He nipped at her neck as he tweaked her nipples and Rachel's knees went weak. Her head fell back against his shoulder and she trusted him to hold her firm.

Then it hit her. She *did* trust him. Implicitly. He'd been there for her every time she'd needed him for the past two weeks. But the more devastating revelation was that she *wanted* him in her life. Not just as an every two days' fuck. She wanted to be with him and talk about his days—both good and bad. And she wanted to talk about her days with him. She didn't really have anyone she could do that with.

One of Dean's hands cupped her pubic area, a single finger sliding into the wetness there. She hadn't cleaned up yet and she had to be soaked. But he certainly didn't seem to mind as he explored her with his long finger. Rachel thought she was done and satisfied, but just that easily he reignited that fire.

When he pulled away without doing more, she growled in frustration. Though she'd come not even ten minutes ago she now wanted more.

Dean chuckled at her expression, dropping a kiss to her

pursed lips. "I'm cold. Let's warm up."

Rachel hadn't realized that *let's warm up* meant screw against the shower wall hard enough to create their own steam. Next time, she would read that glint in his heavenly eyes better.

BUT THE MORE they made love, it seemed like the more they wanted and the more they needed each other. Sensual dreams woke her in the predawn light. When she reached for Dean, he seemed to be waiting for her, mouth smiling and dick hard. Rachel had never been so wrapped up in a man's scent and feel. The sensation of him moving strongly within her, bringing them both immeasurable pleasure, became a drug to her.

It took him a few moments to recover but Rachel enjoyed the time, cradling him to her. When he finally lifted himself off and to the side, he propped his head on his hand to grin at her. "Good morning, beautiful."

"I can't get enough of you," she admitted to him as they separated.

He shrugged and gave her a smile that was chagrined and cheeky. "What can I say? I'm addicting. But believe me, it goes both ways. I had incredible sex with a beautiful woman last night, several times, and slept in her bed, wrapped in her scent. How could I not be hard when I woke up?"

Rachel grinned. Good. If she was going to be plagued by these needs, she was glad he was, too.

They got ready for work together and said goodbye in the driveway, lingering over kisses. Rachel didn't want to let him go, but the emotion seemed mutual.

"Text me later and let's try to get together."

She nodded, more than happy to do that. "Definitely."

"I'll see you later, babe." He paused as if he wanted to say something else, then thought better of it, waved and ducked into the cab of his truck.

Rachel shoved her helmet on her head and swung her leg over the bike seat. The motorcycle roared beneath her as she started it, but it wasn't as satisfying today for some reason. She thought about their goodbye. It seemed incomplete somehow.

An *I love you* from each of them to the other would have finished the conversation. The only thing was that she didn't know if either one of them were ready for that yet.

CHAPTER THIRTEEN

T HEIR RECONNECTION DIDN'T happen that night. Or the next. An emergency contract came down the pipeline and Duncan tapped her to be one of the investigators assigned to it. In Nevada.

As Rachel checked the contents of her emergency go bag, she wondered if she had time to call Dean before she boarded the plane.

Shannon stuck her head in the doorway. "Duncan's looking for you."

Sighing, Rachel flung the bag over her shoulder. She'd have to call him from the airport.

✦   ✦   ✦

DEAN CHECKED HIS phone when he finally had a minute to spare. It had been wall-to-wall crazies today for some reason. Without even looking at a calendar, he could just tell that it was almost a full moon. The crazies always crawled out of the woodwork when the gravitational pull of the earth was lightest.

Damn. He'd missed a call from Rachel. As he pressed the button for voicemail, he grinned, wondering what she would be wearing tonight.

"Hey, Dean, something's come up and I have to go to Nevada for a case." She sighed over the line. "Not sure how long I'll be but I will try to call you at some point. Not even sure what kind of op I'll be on, exactly. Guess we'll have to have our date when I come back. Don't worry. I bought other things at Victoria's Secret." She paused. "I wish I didn't have to leave. Seems like we're just getting to the good part. I'll talk to you as soon as I can. Love you. Bye."

Wait, what?

His heart stuttered in his chest then started to race – 0 to 60 in 2.0 words.

Dean fumbled his phone, trying to remember which button to hit to replay the message. No way. She hadn't said it. He'd just imagined hearing it. Right?

The message started again and he put it on speaker phone. "...talk to you as soon as I can. Love you. Bye."

For the second time in two days she rocked him to his very core. *Love you.* She'd said it. He had absolutely heard it.

Did she even realize she'd said it?

She was so hard to read sometimes. As he was leaving this morning he'd almost told her the same thing. Laughing, he punched the steering wheel of the cruiser, then again. Then he gripped the wheel and yelled into the dash.

Rachel loved him. Just like he loved her.

THREE HOURS LATER, Rachel still couldn't believe she'd said the words out loud. No, she knew exactly why she'd done it. It was because of that damn disjointed, unfinished conversation this morning when she felt like there should have been more.

The *I love you* she'd wanted to say then had slipped out today.

The desert sped by her window. She sat in the back of a Tahoe, on her way to find a woman who had run away from her life. Or maybe it was a bachelorette party. The people that had hired LNF weren't exactly sure. They only knew that they thought she was in Vegas with two of her girlfriends. There had been a fight with the fiancé and she'd stormed off in a huff.

Chad Lowell drove and the new guy, Gabe Carter, sat in the passenger seat. They were a three-man investigation squad looking for three party girls in a city where anonymity was key to everything. Well, no sense in worrying about it before they got there. If the women could be found, they would be the ones to do it.

Rachel had other pressing things on her mind. As she looked down at the cell-phone in her hand, she debated what to do. Should she address the big pink elephant she'd just dropped into their relationship? There was a very good chance Dean hadn't even noticed the little phrase she'd dropped at the end of the voicemail. And he might have taken it as just a generic goodbye.

No, Dean was a sharp cookie and he knew her. There was no chance she would say that and not mean it. And there was no chance that he hadn't heard it.

Maybe—for now—she would act as if it hadn't been said. Then when she got back they could address it if they needed to. The decision wasn't ideal but it would have to do.

The women were harder to find than they'd thought. Yes, they'd been in Vegas. The team found the hotel they'd been staying in using aliases, but after talking to several hotel employees and receiving different stories, they were at a bit of a standstill. Until they talked to Miguel.

Through a series of conversations they were directed to the night shift valet manager, Miguel. "Oh, yes, I remember those girls very well. They tipped like they were millionaires, but you could tell they weren't."

"What do you mean?" Chad asked.

Miguel shrugged, heavy shoulders bunching. "I don't know. They were too nice. It was like they weren't used to the money. The guy they were with, though…he was definitely used to the money. That man probably hasn't said a thank you in his life but he was throwing around the Benjy's like they were tissues."

She and Chad exchanged a glance.

"Do you know the man's name?" Chad asked.

Miguel cocked his head. "Maybe." The he grinned and waited expectantly.

Chad drew his wallet out of his pocket and handed the man a hundred dollar bill. Miguel's gaze lingered on the burn scars on Chad's disfigured left hand for a second before he looked up.

"Oh, yeah," Miguel laughed. "His name was Peter Wattman. That little brunette was hanging all over him."

Shit. The little brunette was their runaway, Misti Cokes. Currently engaged to their employer Jarod White. Rachel drew out her cell and sent off a message to Gabe, who was back in the room following some leads via phone.

"Any idea where they went or when they left?"

Miguel scratched his chin, black bristle scraping. He looked at them apologetically. "Not really."

Chad drew another hundred out of his wallet and handed it over. "Oh, yeah," Miguel made a motion like he'd just remembered. "I think Wattman said something about flying up to his house in the mountains. Very remote. I can check with my driver but I believe he took them to the airstrip."

With a sigh, Chad nodded. "Can you check, please? It's very important that we find this woman."

Out of the goodness of his heart, Miguel didn't charge them for the phone call to his driver. "Yup. He took them to the airport two nights ago. The two women who were with the brunette flew east. The dark haired girl boarded a chopper with

Wattman."

Rachel continued to forward the details to Gabe so he could look for the charter company while they finished up here.

Miguel didn't seem to have any more details so she and Chad headed back to the Tahoe.

"This girl doesn't want to be found," Chad said as they pulled out of the parking lot.

"I don't think so either."

It wasn't hard to track Peter Wattman. The businessman was well-known at the airport because he had his own plane and chartered helicopters regularly. He did business in Silicon Valley but played in Nevada, flying back and forth between the two frequently.

Rachel's gut tightened when she heard that and she wondered if this secluded house was only approachable by helicopter. With her luck it would be.

A text message dinged on her phone from Gabe. *History of sticky entanglements with women he's met on dating sites. Charges filed once for assault then dropped abruptly.*

Great. Rachel held the phone so Chad could see the screen and he winced.

"So, are we just going to walk up to his door and knock?" she asked. "Hey, we're looking for Misti. She ran away from her fiancé. Have you seen her?"

Chad grinned at her. "It may just be that easy. If he took her up there promising one thing and delivering another, she may be ready to head home."

"This guy sounds pervy."

Chad nodded. "I agree. We'll have to play this by ear."

Rachel shook her head. She really hoped the woman wasn't gullible enough to fly two states away, meet a man who promised her the world in a bar on the Vegas strip and leave with him.

Chad aimed his considerable Texas charm at the lone woman manning the reception desk at Henderson Executive Airport. Within minutes he had learned that yes, they'd had helicopter charters to Mr. Wattman's home and that he had been through two nights ago with a dark-haired young woman.

Rachel crossed her arms and wandered away to let him learn what he could and to try to get her nerves under control. She could hear Chad making arrangements for two to fly up there, and they were the only two of them here. They certainly weren't going to drive back to the city to pick up Gabe.

The thought of flying in a helicopter made her sick to her stomach. Impulsively, she pulled out her phone. There was a text message there.

Just thinking about you... That was really nice, but she didn't understand the camel emoticon afterwards.

What is that?

Within a few seconds her screen flashed. *It's a camel! Thought you might need one out there in the desert.*

In spite of her worry, she smiled. *You're too funny! Thanks. I needed that.*

What's up??? Are you ok?

She sighed, debating whether or not to say anything. *Yes. I'm ok. Might have to fly in a few.*

Ohhhh.... Plane?

No.

There was a long pause and she found herself clutching the phone, waiting, praying his words would galvanize her.

I have faith in you, babe. If a job needs to get done, you'll be the one to do it, no matter what.

Then, in big block letters. *I LOVE YOU. You CAN do this.*

Tears blurred her vision as she looked at the conglomeration of letters that meant so much. The *I love you* should have been purple and flashing, because that was all she saw. And amazingly, it did ease her fear of the trip ahead.

"The charter will be here in ten minutes. Are you going to be okay on a chopper?"

She looked up at Chad standing beside her and simply nodded her head.

It wasn't ideal, but she'd known this day would come at some point. Maybe it was better to have it just happen instead of a long build up and time spent planning and worrying.

When the Bell 427 landed on the pad out front, she was hugely reassured. The 427 was a proven combat machine and had been manufactured for years. And this one looked to be top of the line, shining black in the afternoon sun.

In spite of her fears, her heart sped with excitement. Every day for years, as she walked out onto the tarmac to her own ship, excitement had thrummed through her. It didn't matter if she was hauling Marines or Humvees or porta-potties, if it meant she was going to be in the air, it made her happy. And it gave her purpose. She had been damn good at her job.

Chad rested a hand on her shoulder. "Take as much time as you need to."

Damn it. She refused to cry in front of her boss. The two of them had gone through a lot together when they'd protected Lora and Mercy in Texas. She'd watched him fall in love with them and it had shown her anything was possible, even in the worst of circumstances. He was a really good friend now and understood that this was a huge step for her.

She nodded. "Give me a few, okay?"

With a wink he turned and exited to the helicopter pad, where the blades were slowly coming to rest. An older gentleman wearing a black ball cap met him at the side of the machine and shook his hand. They talked for a few minutes before Chad climbed into the passenger compartment. The pilot began a service check, leisurely going from one item to the next. In her mind, Rachel identified every item on her own checklist. Granted, the Super Stallion had been about ten times the size of this craft, but the mechanics and avionics were the same.

Rachel exited the terminal and headed across the pavement. She was Chad's backup. She could do this. It was her job. She had to go.

The older gentleman looked up when she stopped a few feet away. Rachel realized he wore a service hat from Vietnam. "Did you fly in Vietnam, sir?"

His face split into a sad smile. "Yes, ma'am I did. Flew Hueys for many years. I was shot down a couple times too. Your buddy told me you might be anxious about getting on a chopper again, but I promise that this little lady," he patted the side of the 427, "is gentler than anything. What did you operate?"

"The Sikorsky CH-53 Super Stallion for the Marines. Three tours in Iraq and Afghanistan before I put her down hard in the sand. No fatalities, though."

The man nodded once and rested a hand on her shoulder before taking her hand in his own. "That's what matters then. I'm Jack."

"Very nice to meet you, Jack. I'm Rachel."

"I'm going to finish my check before we take off. You take your time. Nose around inside if you want to."

Once again, she was fighting tears. Between Chad, Dean and now Jack she'd found more support in the last hour than she had anywhere else in her life. Suddenly, the thought of going back up into the air didn't seem so scary anymore.

In her job with LNF, domestic flights happened fairly regularly. But flying in a helicopter was definitely out of the ordinary.

Jack turned away to finish his check and Rachel watched him. She remembered doing all this like it was yesterday. She wandered around the machine, conscious of Jack working around her. He should have been done with his pre-fight check by now but he was prolonging it for her sake.

Stepping to the far side of the machine she opened the cockpit door. Oh, wow... much more basic than the Stallion. She could fly this in her sleep.

Then she caught herself. Damn, she was actually thinking of flying again. Not being a passenger... but flying the damn thing herself?

"I don't have a copilot. You're more than welcome to join me up front."

She climbed in without a word, automatically reaching for the headset hanging above her and strapping in. Jack climbed in beside her and did the same, then began the ignition process. The rotor began to spin overhead and the engine whined, but again, it was nothing compared to the Stallion.

Then he drew up on the stick. Her stomach clutched and rolled as they began to pull away from the earth. Rachel held the straps of her harness in her hands, but realized she wasn't especially scared. No, in fact, she was *thrilled*. As Jack flew the helicopter over the terminal and headed toward the south, she leaned into the turn just like she'd always done.

Rachel focused on her body. Nothing on her hurt. Jack had been completely right about the 427 being gentle. Her neck and spine felt completely normal. She laughed internally, knowing that a big happy grin had spread across her face. If she had been flying these, perhaps she could have stayed in the military.

No. The thought brought her up short. No. Everything happened for a reason. If she'd stayed in the military she would never have met Dean. And he was worth everything to her. She thought of the *I love you* he'd sent her. He had heard her slip-up. But he'd responded deliberately, with no prompting from her.

Retrieving her phone from her pocket she looked at the

display. No cell service. She should have known. Well, she could enjoy the flight at least.

They flew for twenty minutes into a desolate, rocky area. As they continued, Rachel was strongly reminded of Afghanistan's harsh landscape. And then Jack motioned to the left. A monolithic, monochromatic terra-cotta colored house jutted up out of the rocks. There was a road winding up into the hills to the house, but Jack had said he flew Wattman in and out. Driving probably took a very long time to get anywhere. And there didn't appear to be any other houses or buildings around. The guy was totally secluded out here.

Rachel felt a spasm of anxiety as Jack positioned the chopper to land, but he was so competent that they touched down with barely a whisper. Any tension she'd felt evaporated as he turned to her with a rakish grin. Rachel put her fist out with an answering smile and he bumped her knuckles as he started to shut down the chopper.

Rachel hopped down out of the cockpit, grinning. Chad gave her considering look and a good slap on the back, then they turned to the paver path leading to the house. They could celebrate her victory later.

CHAPTER FOURTEEN

✦

M ISTI COKES DIDN'T come running out of the house screaming for rescue. No, she just stomped. She slammed the front door behind her and marched away from the house; before they'd made it down the path to the house she was halfway to them. It was easy to identify her from the photos they'd been given but she now sported a shiner and a split lip, still freshly bleeding.

"I need you to fly me out of here. I don't know who you are, but the man that lives here is a jackass and I plan on filing charges against him. If you don't take me out of here I'll file charges against you, too for not helping me."

Her big blue eyes filled with tears and she crossed her arms over her breasts, quivering with equal parts fury and fright.

Chad held his palm up. "There's no need for that, Ms. Cokes. We've been looking for you."

The petite woman broke into sobs then, and let Chad wrap an arm around her shoulders to walk away from the house.

A tall man in ragged jeans and a gray Pink Floyd t-shirt jogged out of the house. "Misti, wait, honey."

Was *this* Peter Wattman? An overgrown kid?

Chad glanced back but continued up the path to the helicopter. He made a spinning motion in the air and Jack began to wind the engine.

Wattman started to jog after Misti, but Rachel stepped into his path. "Back off, Mr. Wattman."

"I don't know who you people are but you're trespassing. My girlfriend and I were just getting ready to sit down to lunch."

"I'm not your fucking girlfriend, you damn whack job," Misti screamed. Then she clambered into the passenger compartment of the 427.

Wattman tried to follow her but Rachel blocked his way, holding her palms up. Wattman's bloodshot eyes turned mean and he reared his right hand over his left shoulder for a back-hand swing, but Rachel saw it coming a mile away. She blocked the slap then stepped into his space, ramming a hard palm up under his chin. His teeth snapped shut and he staggered back and fell on his ass, looking stunned.

Rachel turned and jogged to the helicopter. She climbed into the cockpit and strapped in. As Jack lifted them up and away, she took pictures of Wattman and the house with her cellphone. She didn't know if she would need them or not, but better to be safe than sorry.

RACHEL GAINED A little more respect for Misti after they flew her away. The woman broke down a little bit but controlled it by the time they landed. It was obvious she was listening to Chad as he explained who they were and who had hired them.

There was very little anxiety landing this time, Rachel noted. Jack had been as good as his word and put them down softer than she could have imagined. As she was unstrapping he pulled a business card from a central cubby and handed it to her.

"I'm not staying—I have to get to another charter—but if you need anything let me know." His kind eyes flicked to Chad and Misti walking toward the terminal. "If that little girl wants to press charges I can do up a witness statement that she was fine when I flew her out there two days ago."

Rachel took the card and nodded. "Thanks, Jack. I'll let you know."

She started to move again but he put a hand on her arm. "And if you ever want to go up again, or maybe get your hand on the stick, you let me know. I own this company and I'm in Denver fairly frequently. Or you can come out here if you're more comfortable in the desert. I have a few toys you can pick from."

Rachel's chest tightened at the incredible gift he was offering and it took her a moment to speak. "Thank you, sir. That would be an honor."

Impulsively she reached across the console and hugged him. And as she stood beneath the desert sun, basking in the stinging rotor wash as he lifted off, she had a very strong feeling she would be coming back here.

THEY DROVE THE Tahoe to the hotel to collect Carter and grab their bags. They also called the police so that the assault on her could be documented.

Rachel stood against the wall as Misti talked to the cops. Basically, she'd gotten cold feet. With her wedding fast approaching, she'd felt like a noose was tightening around her neck. Grabbing her two best friends they'd bolted for Las Vegas. Peter Wattman had approached them at a show, lavished money on them and made life exciting again. He had told Misti how amazing she was and that he could take care of her better than the guy in Colorado. Misti had fallen for it. Wattman had paid for the girlfriends to go home and Misti had flown away to his exotic desert hideaway…which had no cell phone service and a password protected wifi. Misti had been at his mercy.

"He changed as soon as we were alone. Promised he would take care of me but refused to let me do anything. But then he would turn on the charm and things would be easy again. I slept with him once consensually, but then he tried to force himself on me and I fought. I heard the helicopter outside and I bashed him on the head with a salad bowl. Then these guys came."

She smiled up at Rachel and Rachel smiled back. Damn the kid was young. Rachel was glad she hadn't spent any more time on the tarmac when they left though. It could have turned out much worse for Misti.

Vegas PD documented her injuries, took Jack's information down and promised that charges would proceed.

"Let's go home, kids," Chad told them, grabbing his duffle. "Maybe I can still read my little girl a bedtime story."

They piled into the Tahoe and hustled to catch the flight Carter had booked out of McCarran International Airport.

Her phone buzzed.

You're killing me. What happened?

All is good. Running to catch flight home. Meet me at my house at 10?

YES!!!

CHAPTER FIFTEEN

✦

R ACHEL MADE IT home with a half hour to spare but Dean was already there waiting for her.

Pulling the bike into the garage, she removed her helmet and hung it from the throttle. Then she turned and stepped into his open arms.

Dean smelled of laundry softener and good, clean man. Rachel couldn't get enough of him.

Pulling back he grinned down at her. "You look so good to me. I see you and my heart melts."

Chuckling, she shook her head at him. "Whatever..."

He cocked his head, giving her a severe look and she rolled her eyes.

"Fine, even though I haven't showered or brushed my helmet head, I'm beautiful to you."

"You are," he whispered, bending to press a kiss to her lips.

Rachel sank into him, loving the feel of being cradled in his arms. It had only been a few days but it seemed longer. Already her body was readying for him. And it was obvious that he was ready for her.

"Let's move this inside."

Dean peered beneath her hair. "You still have the earrings on."

"Of course. I love them. Nobody has ever given me anything like them before."

Dean grinned. "And nobody better now, either," he growled. "But me."

Rachel shut the garage door and led the way into the house. Grunt met them at the door, howling furiously for more food. Rachel threw a handful of food in the bowl, but it was a little difficult because Dean was reaching for the button of her pants. He'd already tugged up her t-shirt and unfastened her bra.

She giggled as she navigated her way to the bedroom, swatting at his hands. It didn't matter. She was as bare as she could be without stopping to shed her boots. Collapsing to the mattress she ripped at her laces, desperate to have them off. Dean was shucking his own clothes and only had to kick off his tennis shoes. Then, as she struggled with the damned laces, he was fondling her breasts and ran a line of kisses up her back.

Finally, she was free of everything and turned to him. He immediately fell back on the bed with her sprawled across him. Rachel spread her thighs across his hips and sat up.

"Oh," he sighed, his bright gaze running over her. "You're going to get tired of hearing this but you are stunning. I love your breasts. I love your strength. I could look at you forever."

Rachel leaned down to press a kiss to his lips. "Thank you."

Dean wrapped his arms around her, sitting up easily in spite of their combined weight. He looked her in the eye and cradled her head in his hands. "I'm completely in love with you, Rachel. Not just one thing but everything about you. My heart recognizes you as its other half. I knew when I stopped at that crash that something big was happening when I talked to you. You showed such courage sitting in that mangled mess. And you show courage in so many ways every day. I wish I had been there to see you climb in that helicopter."

Rachel laughed, but it came out more as a sob. "It was amazing," she whispered, her throat tight. "This entire day has been amazing. You know I love you, too. I don't have the words like you do but I will forever be there for you. I am so amazed at what has happened between us. I never expected to find anything like it."

Dean pulled her close, his arms secure around her. "Then I'm going to tell you how much I love you five hundred times a day, until you believe it."

She laughed lightly, her head nestled against his chest. "I'm going to hold you to that."

Then she began nibbling his skin. She rocked her hips against the erection she could feel between them. Doing a little maneuvering, she guided him inside her, sank down and wrapped her legs around his hips. Then they rocked together, mouths fused, hearts beating in time. Rachel bore down, loving the feel of the orgasm rolling toward her. Dean held her hips in his hands, forcing her down against his body. Rachel panted and cried out, convulsing in his arms. His own orgasm struck suddenly and he cried out, burrowing his face in her hair. Then, unable to hold them up any longer, he rocked to his back with her on top of him.

"I love you, Rachel."

"And I love you, Dean."

EVERY HOUR HE fell more in love with her. It was one a.m. and they sat at the kitchen table noshing on snacks. Rachel was recounting her day as she stroked Grunt.

"I think I want to fly again," she admitted.

Dean laughed. "You've always wanted to fly, whether you admitted it to yourself or not. I could see that the day I picked you up from the hospital."

She sighed, propping her head on her hand. "Yes, I think you're right. I just didn't want to be disappointed if it wasn't as amazing as I remembered it. But when Jack pulled us up into the air, I got that same feeling in my gut. That same excitement."

Her golden eyes swam with a glorious light and Dean knew he would move heaven and earth to keep that light burning. "Then I vote that we call Jack soon, just to get you back into the air."

Rachel laughed, nodding. "That we will do. Thank you, Dean."

He shook his head. "Don't thank me. Just love me."

Her eyes turned serious. "I do, completely. More than I ever thought possible. I will always be thankful it was you who stopped that day. As soon as I saw your sexy eyes everything else just faded away. I thought I had dreamed them," she sighed. "Then you came to the hospital and I couldn't believe it. When I look into your eyes, it's like a different kind of flying. It makes me more complete than anything else in the world."

She leaned over the table and he met her halfway, his throat tight with emotion. That was one of the most eloquent things he'd ever heard his former Marine say. "I love you, Rachel, and I'll fly with you anytime."

Grinning, she kissed him as if he were her every tomorrow. And if he had anything to say about it, he would be.

The End...

If you would like to read about the 'combat modified' veterans of the **Lost and Found Investigative Service**, check out these books:

The Embattled Road

Embattled Hearts – Book 1

Embattled Minds – Book 2

Embattled Home – Book 3

Embattled SEAL – Book 4

Her Forever Hero – Grif

SEAL's Lost Dream – Flynn

Unbreakable SEAL – Max

Embattled Christmas

Reclaiming the SEAL

Loving Lilly

Other books by J.M. Madden

A Touch of Fae

Second Time Around

A Needful Heart

Wet Dream

Love on the Line Book 1

Love on the Line Book 2

The Awakening Society

Tempt Me

Urban Moon Anthology

If you'd like to connect with me on social media and keep updated on my releases, try these links:

Newsletter: jmmadden.com/newsletter/

Website: www.jmmadden.com

Facebook: facebook.com/jmmaddenauthor

Twitter: @authorjmmadden

Tsū: tsu.co/JMMadden

And of course you can always email me at authorjmmadden@gmail.com

About the Author

NY Times and USA Today Bestselling author J.M. Madden writes compelling romances between 'combat modified' military men and the women who love them. J.M. Madden loves any and all good love stories, most particularly her own. She has two beautiful children and a husband who always keeps her on her toes.

J.M. was a Deputy Sheriff in Ohio for nine years, until hubby moved the clan to Kentucky. When not chasing the family around, she's at the computer, reading and writing, perfecting her craft. She occasionally takes breaks to feed her animal horde and is trying to control her office-supply addiction, but both tasks are uphill battles. Happily, she is writing full-time and always has several projects in the works. She also dearly loves to hear from readers! So, drop her a line. She'll respond.

63537645R00078

Made in the USA
Lexington, KY
11 May 2017